The Secrets of Mt. Sumagang

A Novel

ABE N. MARGALLO

"If you love Sumagang, then it is not extinct. If you don't, then it is. Kaput. Dead. It's just how we look at it. It's all in your heart."

Contact: **abemargallo@yahoo.com**

Printed in the United States by:
Lulu Press, Inc.
3101 Hillsborough St.
Raleigh, NC 27607
Ordering Information: via **www.lulu.com/red**
ISBN: 978-0-578-15622-4

Cover design by Mel Margallo and Karla Margallo

For

the **"GUYS"**

of

Iriga

Acknowledgements

I am delightedly indebted to several people during the writing of this novel. First, my wife, Jenny, who had reviewed the initial chapters and thought the imagery so far was "quite impressive" and thus egged me on to finish it. My brother, Daldo, who has given the wise counsel to keep the story fictional, rather than historical. My children, Karla and Andrew, who have taken time looking for misspelled words, weird syntax and other grammatical sore spots and helped improve the book's final form. Finally, Grace Cobin, my mother-in-law, the first to read the unedited copy in toto and in one sitting because while not acquiescent with my politics she has found the story's two leading characters "very real."

I wish to apologize to my town for the liberties I have taken of its sophistication.

The
Secrets of
Mt. Sumagang

A Novel

ABE N. MARGALLO

CHAPTER 1

The devout sat quietly on the mahogany pews. The Y-riga parish priest speckled his homily with broken English, two Bikol dialects and a perfect Spanish. It was midsummer of 1957.

After reading the Gospel, the priest returned to the first reading:

Those who are in the flesh cannot please God.
But you are not in the flesh;
    on the contrary, you are in the spirit,
    if only the spirit of God dwells in you.
Whoever does not have the Spirit of Christ
    does not belong to him.

The elderly prelate was incoherent, as always, with his explication of the biblical readings and befuddled more the Sunday congregants whenever he also mixed his Spanish with Latin. Speaking now in Y-riga and Naga dialects, he abruptly changed the subject to church dress code (for women) and then to the church finances that's ever in bad shape. That instant is always opportune for the latecomers to sneak in. Ordinary folks who come late to church are assumed to be late for a reason. Even so, they tiptoe to the side with their heads lowered to find any available seat.

But the town's matrons are late because they are supposed to. Today, as usual, their grand entrance was followed by a steady and rapid stride on the center aisle to the combined disgust, admiration and envy of more than a few souls.

The Y-riga church is typical of most churches in provincial Philippines. It is *the* Church. Not just any church. Although perched like a medieval castle in the center of the town proper, its physical realm (as late as the 50s) included nothing more than the old convent and the parochial school cramped together on the elevated churchyard. As a piece of prime realty, the setting, as any other catholic parish in the country, was strategic: a stone's throw from the municipal hall, the market place, the town plaza, the Y-riga Hotel, the train station, the Chinese grocery and hardware store, the Armand and Rosa movie houses and the town's two colleges.

The elevation of the church estate at the heart of the town perpetuated a sense that the Spanish friars had once held full sway in the town. The feeling was truer among older folks on whom the *separation of church and state* seemed to have never rubbed off, or perhaps they have never really gotten the whole shebang since their American mentors bequeathed them the doctrine at the beginning of the last century. To these folks, whatever had beclouded their long-held traditions during the bygone Castillian era would get settled after every local election: the municipal officials came and went, but the same clergy had to bestow blessings on each set of newly chosen officials. The exclusion in the ritual of minority sects was a given.

Mrs. Ymelda Monteverde, the austere yet comely public school teacher, fumbled the rosary beads in prayerful murmurs. She seemed unaware the town mayor seated from across the left wing of the church was stealing a few glances at her, although most of the time he was staring blank at the overly ornate altar. Mrs. Monteverde was however only pretending not to notice the entrance of the matrons when daughter Rebecca gave her away. The little mischief was imitating the sounds produced by the high-heeled shoes with a playful "tik tak tik tak" when the mother cut her off rather audibly. The rhythmic noise would be broken by the pretense to make a lighter, slower pace whenever the priest paused, somewhat grudgingly, in his sermon. Rebecca would notice the shift in cadence and snigger. Then, the older women folks who preferred to be seated close to the altar slid aside in unison to the far end of the pew as the bejeweled and heavily perfumed entrants stopped to exercise their front-row privileges.

I took my shower very early this morning, why couldn't these people? *Punyeta!* Barely budging, Mrs. Monteverde swore, and held on to her spot. Then she raised her hands with the rosary to her forehead and bowed, eyes closed, her lips moving more noticeably.

"Ma, you said something?"

"Shh." She was ostensibly stern this time.

Rebecca kneeled down, mimicking the piousness of her mother.

Churchgoing is not a family affair in Y-riga. The women with the little ones hear mass inside the church while the men, in their Sunday outfits, suits or *barong Tagalog*, stay behind, standing by the main doorway during the entire mass practically blocking the entrance. It's convenient for the men that way to just take a few steps outside, out of the sight of the Presider, at the start of the homily. The intermission is taken as a matter of course to allow for a brief socialization with peers, for petty chatters about politics or the hot news of the day. It's been a practice certainly not out of irreverence but possibly only because of some supposition that the homily is not an essential part of the mass, that the men couldn't follow the biblical references because they don't read the bible anyway, that persistent pleas for charities are unwelcome or that the dress code breach concerns only the women.

The men will punctually return to their posts when someone announces the sermon is over.

This time, Leo Monteverde and another neatly suited up fellow tarried longer outside.

"Did you learn of the news yet, Prof?" Leo asked the fellow in whisper.

"Yep. Bloody gruesome. The poor bastard was decapitated and mutilated. Seems like old times, Leo," Prof. Salvador Palma replied. "Warlito, the mayor's brother, may be into it," he added with a bit of resignation.

"No, new signs of the times, Sal. It makes me really worry, my friend."

The conversation in an unusually grave undertone went on until the consecration bell.

For many of the overworked farmers and the workingmen who have nothing to put on but work clothes, the wives make the Sunday indulgences in their behalf. The youngsters on the other hand, the boys in particular, attend the mass as though by force of habitude, band with their crew too, and like to be where the men are to feel like men. They have not known any other parish priest but Padre Lazaro, now simply Monsignor to most of the townspeople that still revere him like the friar of the old. Not the two little rascals, Salvio and Minandro.

"He's gay, definitely. Look how he gestures with his left hand," Salvio whispered to his buddy.

Minandro grinned but didn't say a word, if only for the fact that he would be more recognizable as a Monteverde to churchgoers and any palpable misdeed inside the church would easily come to the knowledge of his mother, Ymelda, who was seated in the front row with Rebecca, his "little sister."

The rambling sermon of Monsignor made the two boys impatient, half of the parishioners drowsy. Now, the electric fan was not working on their pew and the monotony of the voice coming out of the lousy sound system and poor acoustics made unbearable the humid air trapped inside the church on that summer afternoon.

Salvio and Minandro winked at each other and quickly rose to skip the rest of the homily, and then sneaked up to the church belfry.

CHAPTER 2

There were already four other boys in the church tower busy wagering in a coin game of *cara y cruz.*

"Walk straight, don't look at them," Minandro ordered his buddy.

"Alright."

The young gamesters ignored the two anyway.

Salvio and Minandro proceeded to climb to the higher section of the belfry which provided the best panoramic view of the town center against the magnificent backdrop of Mt. Sumagang. It's been their favorite spot where many a time they have woven one tale after another about the majesty of the mountain, like some wise storytellers. Often they'd forget climbing down to finish hearing mass. But now, they were just interested in how a flag planted on the peak of *iliyan* would look like from where they stood.

Minandro gazed absorbedly far afield. The sky's so clear today; we could get as close to it as from a distance just like this if only we brought our binoculars, he mused. Then his concentration turned fierce as of a hawk ready to pounce on its prey.

"Are you okay?"

Minandro did not answer. Salvio is used to that demeanor of his friend when engrossed with something.

Iliyan lies at the lower crest of Sumagang. It is certainly far taller than any of the hillocks in the wilds of *kadlagan,* the boys' forest playground in the lowlands bordering the backyard of Salvio's house, but in the bosom of her imposing mother, iliyan looks no more than a molehill from a distance as far as the church belfry, about three or four miles away. For a week now, the boys have been planning to conquer the minute monster in what had once been a primal jungle. There's not much to contend for in the backwoods of kadlagan where they learned how to climb the *balaigang* tree, made their first kill, overcome their worst fears and lost their boyhood.

The duo attempted to climb iliyan last summer almost by impulse. They were then harvesting wild Java guava on the foot of the hill when they challenged each other to climb it. After hours of trekking up starting at about noontime, they became exhausted, dehydrated and famished. They had nothing in terms of provisions but a couple of ripened guavas stacked up on one side of their trousers' pockets. The other pocket was filled with selection of stones from *brookside*, the brook by the side of the highway, serving as their slingshot bullets.

Through the *cogon* twice as tall as them, the youthful adventurers would gaze down every so often during the climb to scale their feat, and also to delight themselves with the emerging vista of the entire town of Y-riga. The higher they went, the further the town's horizon loomed, like a landscape being rendered in reverse by some mysterious strokes emanating from the mountains. But the sun was punishing their exposed napes, causing them continually to perspire, which was bad for the rubber bands of their weapons of choice slung around their necks. The thin shadows of some dwarf coconut trees lining the trail were barely providing any relief as the sun rose to its zenith at mid-noon during that time of the summer. But the mountain breeze was a blessing, and when the wind blew stronger, the cogon would whistle a song and dance with it, the *mayas* join the impromptu ensemble when roused from their nests, and if the climbers took a brief respite, the whole rhythm would have lulled them to sleep. Yet they went on, and on, and after more than an hour of nonstop climb their legs started to hurt. Salvio began to worry. Minandro too, but it's got to be Salvio to break the unwelcome word that it's time to stop and head back home. Minandro won't do it.

On the way down, Salvio thought he recognized the church below because of the belfry but he did not want to mention it since he was sure Minandro would debate with him on that issue. Besides, they didn't have the energy and the luxury of time to indulge in any argument the way they usually do at the church belfry.

It was way past twilight when they reached the plain. Past dinner time too.

CHAPTER 3

He's a late-bloomer, Mrs. Ymelda Monteverde would tell her co-teachers. Minandro didn't learn how to speak until he was three years old. He was however a portly little baby Buddha compared to Antonio, his elder brother.

Mrs. Monteverde once entered the three-month old Minandro in a healthy baby contest sponsored by the town's Puericulture Center. Baby Minandro bagged the second prize plus five pesos and the brief stardom has made the frail-looking Antonio conscious of his physical frame ever since.

As a toddler, Minandro was fairer in complexion and chink-eyed, and delighted Mr. Kiong, the Chinese owner of the bakery in front of the church. Anyone, with little Minandro tagging along, would get an extra *pan de sal* or *pan de coco* whenever a purchase was made from Mr. Kiong himself. Antonio started calling his younger sibling Kiong Fu because of it, especially every time they had a fight.

Now, at 12, Minandro has lost the baby flab, but was still chinky, and way fairer than his buddy. He was however just about an inch taller than Salvio who was two years his junior. He's a late-bloomer, Mrs. Monteverde would insist to anyone curious to ask, sometimes as an excuse when comparison was drawn by folks between Minandro and Antonio, particularly in terms of school achievements. No sooner, the label has carried a positive ring since it has now come out quite casually from a mother held by town mates in high respect as a pedagogue.

When they are very sweet to each other, Salvio calls Minandro, LB meaning "late-bloomer" and Salvio because of his darker skin tone gets in return an endearing "Hawaiian Boy" tag from his friend or HB, for short, to even off the convenience of abbreviation. Otherwise, they call each other "guy," just as everyone else in the town would call each other. Guy means buddy in Y-riga.

"Guy, we have to start at least by five in the morning next time," Salvio was trying to convince Minandro. "If we went as far as halfway last week, we could make it if we start earlier, and still not be late for dinner," Salvio continued as he leaned forward on the moss-coated balustrades of the belfry. Minandro agreed with Salvio's calculation without saying a word, just by being absorbed by the challenge in front of them. And then, he mumbled something to himself.

One story goes that dinosaurs had roamed like humans in Mt. Sumagang which today overlays the lowlands that were carved out into four townships by the Spanish friars. There was constant strife among the giant creatures for dominance but the few that had survived the deadly wars were blown to extinction during the mountain's last great eruption. Sumagang blasted off half of itself on the northern side spewing out one mammoth fireball that also dug up a lake. The towns of Banahaw on the north, Bantog on the east and Bua on the west have thus been condemned to endure the wretched disfigurement of Sumagang because of the eruption. This probably explains why the inhabitants of all three towns today are known to feel closer to the presence nearby of the still well-formed Mt. Isarog. Another fiery boulder was ejected in the opposite direction but skipped Y-riga and where it landed sprang an even larger lake, one township away from the majestic and world-renowned Mt. Mayon. Spared by Sumagang's rage, only Y-riga lying south of the mountain is proud today to claim her as its very own. The gorgeous visage of Y-riga's natural wonder has been preserved for the Y-rigueños although only in its near perfect half-cone.

Nonsense! Salvio remembered Mrs. Monteverde cutting him abruptly as he tried to recount the legend to his classmates. The day's assignment for the fourth-grade science class of Mrs. Monteverde was about the wild and giant ferns that are supposed to thrive in the mountain. Salvio brought to class some of the most unique species of the plants, unique but not the giant varieties. The wild ferns had actually been brought down from the higher elevation of the mountain by the workers of Don Patricio. They were mostly aboriginal *Aetas*, or *Agtas* as they are more popularly known to the locals. It was Don Patricio who retold the story to his youngest son Salvio during dinner the night before, with the plants as their main topic for conversation. These plants are really out of the ordinary, Salvio recalled his father explaining to him, but they are not the ones an Y-rigueño still living has yet to see.

Salvio that Sunday morning at the belfry tried to tell his father's account to Minandro partly to take a veiled swipe at Mrs. Monteverde. But Minandro was quite focused at the moment on a sight far beyond iliyan. Salvio began to feel a bit chilly about his buddy's demeanor. It was that look Minandro wore when he had made the first bird kill with his slingshot in kadlagan. The tiny *malapaga*, after absorbing the stone bullet that was bigger than its head, fell deep into a thick grove of bamboos. Minandro was so resolute to retrieve his hunt it took the two of them nearly half of the day cutting through the thicket with a bolo borrowed from the nearest neighbor. The proud shot who led the find came out badly bruised in both hands, in fact bleeding from cuts by the freshly sliced bamboos. But the elation on his face was beyond description when he finally got hold of the dead bird, already beginning to stiffen.

14

Salvio now remembered that during the abortive climb he had seen Mt. Sumagang as being too far off from iliyan contrary to the illusion of proximity offered by sheer distance from the belfry. Before the climb, both of them had always theorized that by sliding down the back side of the hillock they would land right into the bosom of the mother lode. Not right, Salvio concluded. They would end up right back to the jump-off point by just doing that. That's why Salvio saw no point trying to reach the peak of iliyan to scale Sumagang.

Arguing with himself, Salvio thought at least the next time they have a goal: to plant a flag on top of iliyan. Maybe not a crowning achievement but still some serious reason with which to make an impression to the kids on the other side of the tower, and controvert any notion of them as being too wimpy to play *cara y cruz* during Sunday mass.

"Let's just walk home with Frankie and the guys and save our tricycle money," Salvio suggested after church.

Minandro nodded.

Along the highway, Frankie fired his slingshot at a kingfisher resting on a culm of wild grass by the brook. He missed by a mile and the gang heckled at him. Efren took a shot and missed by a feather. The gang roared.

As they ambled past brookside, Salvio playfully recalled something to Minandro on seeing the dried carrion of two *kikig*, the water snakes that must have been run over twenty times by motor vehicles.

"Remember this same spot after our first communion?"

"Yeah," Minandro, a bit embarrassed, grinned without showing his teeth.

"Remember you spat out right here when a BITRANCO bus crushed a kikig into bloody bits and pieces, and then I said you can't do that after communion and before eating something solid—"

Minandro's grin became wider, his eyes even sparkling.

"And you decided to lick your spittle because our catechist, Ms. Matubis, said that's what we should do, lick back the *Santo Forma* from the ground or go to hell?" Salvio was laughing.

"It was dumb."

"Dumb, because you don't believe Ms. Matubis anymore?"

"Do you?"

CHAPTER 4

The Monteverde residence in San Nicolas is eye-catching to any passerby who is not from Y-riga. It is the only one lying far back, about 200 yards from the national highway. The rest of the houses and a few stores and small shops, practically abut the asphalted roadway separated only by a narrow creek on one side and a man-made ditch on the other.

Two giant *kalachuchis*, with their crowns partially fused and forming an arch, serve as the main gate leading through a dirt walkway to the two-story and wood-framed house. When in bloom, the sweet-smelling flowers of the kalachuchis first greet everyone entering the property.

The walkway is wide enough to allow a car to pass and winds a couple of times. A variety of yearlong fruit-bearing trees marks the property boundary lines. The whole landscape is masterfully dotted with an array of tress, palms and plants with low-hanging fruits and orchids of different colors and shapes bundled in coconut husks and dangling from just the right branches. Such a display in arboreal art blends with the wild ferns and grass on the ground, on both sides of the walkway, and the accent of the heavy green of indigenous vines crawling up on one concrete portion of the walls, all bestowing the front yard with a natural terrain of wilderness.

The backyard is even wilder, deeply forested and unbounded.

From the veranda of the house overlooking the garden, the highway and the main BITRANCO bus terminal right across the street, the church belfry a couple of miles southward can be seen if not for the spotted cover of an old *santol* tree. But the open room often reeks of guano manure that Rebecca can't stand. She learned from the housemaids who collect the droppings for garden fertilizer that those "little vampires" prefer to roost upside down during the day in the partly cleaved ceiling of the *balcon*. The porch is connected to what Rebecca fondly calls the family room in the upper floor. On the east side of the house, the peak of Mt. Sumagang is visible, particularly from the window of the *boys' room* immediately adjacent to the veranda.

Don Patricio Bartolome walked past the gate and inhaled, in two deep and quick successions, the sweet scent that greeted him. His eyes were all over the place in muted admiration, and as he approached the house he caressed with the tips of his fingers the ripened *chicos*. He looked around once more to enjoy the landscape before knocking.

The door is made of massive *narra* and has ornate engravings, and one who has not been in the Monteverde residence before would be disappointed not to see more of such an artifact inside. Not Don Patricio anymore who has been a visitor of the house many times before. He just went in, the door being unlocked, and helped himself get seated on the rattan chair near the banistered stairway, the main attraction in the living room.

The silence inside that welcomed the guest was short-lived. It was soon broken by the noise coming out from the backyard, obviously the voices of maids laundering clothes, the splash of water on the ground and the occasional pumping of a deep well.

"Are they upstairs?" the visitor asked one of the maids who just came in through the kitchen door.

She nodded shyly to affirm, without making eye contact.

This armrest needs repair. Don Patricio returned his attention to what's inside the house.

He noticed several cracked tiles badly mislaid on the concrete floors. An antic drawer is set against a plywood wall, otherwise blank but for a grocery calendar hanging from it. Atop the drawer are the kindergarten graduation pictures of Antonio and Rebecca and a baby picture of Minandro. Don Patricio never really bothered asking any time before why Minandro's graduation picture is missing.

The marks of a dismantled room, now serving as the dining nook opposite the kitchen, are still conspicuous from the pavement. The living room, recently opened up, stretches out wall-to-wall, basically constituting the entire high-ceiling ground floor, except for the makeshift maid's quarters partly separating it from the bathroom.

It just needs a new set of furniture, the wall paints must be evenly applied, and this could be rich a man's house, Don Patricio began critiquing the place again, comparing it in his subconscious to his own dwelling. He had this thought and then realized that the two slats of the wood jalousie of the living room windows have been missing still since his last visit.

The scenic sight of iliyan was evident through the broken blind and staring at it, a sudden twinge of nostalgia set in on the visitor. To idle the mood away, Don Patricio picked up an old *Journal of Education* lying on the unvarnished coffee table, and began flipping the pages to look for some pictures that might be of interest. It wasn't working so he pulled out from the pocket of his trousers something to fuel him, a betel nut pouch. Then, he made a quid, first by splitting the green nut, then sprinkling it with lime and finally wrapping it with a fresh pepper leaf. He placed one cut in his mouth like a piece of chocolate cube and began chewing. After munching for some time, he headed to the door to spit outside the red juice in his mouth but the sound of footsteps from the stairway aborted his intentions.

"Kumusta, *Padi*,[1]" Mrs. Monteverde greeted the visitor. He showed his horse teeth.

---

[1] *Padi or Pading*: Short for compadre or godfather

CHAPTER 5

The figure emerging from the stairway was the same woman Don Patricio had known some 25 years ago. In her late thirties, the natural good looks of Ymelda, atypically Y-rigueño, were unharmed by three childbirths or by more than a decade of service in the public school system, explaining in turn her many pedagogic mannerisms. The traces of Chinese, Spanish and Malay in her countenance all counted up to an innate parochial elegance. If anything, whenever she asserted herself, her once simple speech would evince certain churlishness owing as much to years of post-graduate pursuits as her marital companionship with Leo Monteverde, a former World War II guerilla leader and self-described thinker.

"Your *Pading* Leo stayed late last night working on his book," Mrs. Monteverde said somewhat apologetically.

"Hmm," Don Patricio replied preferring not to open his mouth to hide his dyed teeth.

He rushed past the woman of the house to head towards the door and spat out what he couldn't hold in his mouth. The unwanted red saliva hit the orchid hanging from the guava tree and scared away a couple of birds. Mrs. Monteverde pretended not to see what happened. Don Patricio returned to the rattan chair and practically flaunted his mismatched rubber sandals by crossing his legs.

"Minandro and your godson are at home, *Mading*[2] Ymelda."

"I thought so, Padi. I didn't hear them in the backyard this morning."

"*Madi*, I had this telegram from my son Esteban last night," Don Patricio quickly changed the topic, wanting to cut further pleasantries. "He needs me to wire 150,000 pesos for him to take the finals," he continued.

Mrs. Monteverde surmised what's coming next.

"You can have my remaining property east of iliyan. It has more and better coconut trees. Just let me harvest the pineapples in two weeks; I need this one for our travel expenses to Manila. The whole family plans to join the trip. You know there are tenants living in the plantation, 30 or 40 families, the rest are Aetas who actually live in Sumagang. Pading Leo can prepare the deed of sale. I really don't mind. Besides—"

---

[2] *Madi or mading*: Feminine form for *padi* or *pading*

23

"Is your Esteban certain to graduate this month?" Mrs. Monteverde asked in a way that the interruption to Patricio's monologue was still polite.

"Yes, but he must be allowed to take his finals first. He doesn't want to lose his slot at Gen. Luna Hospital. All the medical graduates want to intern there and he was among those who made the first cut."

"Oh my, little Esteban will be a physician very soon. How time flies! That means we are not getting any younger either. Dr. Esteban Bartolome, doesn't it sound wonderful, Padi?"

That last question from Mrs. Monteverde wetted the eyes of her visitor. He turned around to hide them and yet the image of iliyan through the broken blind reasserted itself despite being blurred by tears.

Mrs. Monteverde, though outwardly sympathetic, was hardly moved by Don Patricio's comportment. She had conjured up this scenario many times and right now her thoughts were wandering about the real prospect of owning 800 hectares of coconut and pineapple plantation, a *hacienda* for all intents and purposes. Attached to the huge landholdings would be the distinguished title of matron, just like Mrs. Alfonso, Mrs. Tan, Mrs. Magistrado, Mrs. Alvarez and all of them who come to church late, heavily perfumed and bejeweled, and take the front-row pews as a matter of privilege. Now she pictured herself as going to the town center's grocery, instead of the wet market, with uniformed maids tagging along carrying huge baskets. She would get an invitation to join the Daughters of Isabella and don those distinctive blue uniforms, receive the special red envelope from Monsignor, and invitations to weddings, anniversaries, and other important town occasions all because she's Mrs. Monteverde. Watch this simple pedagogue show her dancing skills in the town's grand balls. Right now, she's also thinking of throwing a big party in the Monteverde residence for Antonio's graduation next April. The house has to be repainted, she imagined.

"300,000 pesos Madi, if you add the balance from the last time," Don Patricio rather insolently transformed Ymelda's daydreaming to the stark what ifs.

What if Leo's book deal fell through and the publisher withheld the advance payment? What if Leo had his fits and didn't recover fast enough to finish the final manuscript on time? Even then, the publisher committed only 200,000 pesos. Where would the rest come from if it has taken them nearly five years to stash 30,000 pesos under Rebecca's mattress to enroll Antonio for college? And what if Don Patricio offered the property to Mrs. Tan or to Mr. Kiong's wife?

"Padi, I will need to have a word with your Padi. I'll send Minandro for you as soon as Leo and I made up our minds, maybe tonight or tomorrow morning, if you don't mind."

Don Patricio left the Monteverde residence knowing fully well that losing the last piece of his iliyan properties would mean losing as much those precious possessions as his own being. He has more landholdings on the other side of the mountain but it's the expanse of his iliyan plantation the townspeople point to as the Hacienda Bartolome that made a Don out of a no-read-no-write farmer. People could be very cruel sometimes. And they will be, he thought, sooner than later.

Don Patricio went straight to iliyan to explain his plan to Isko, the chief of the Agtas in the settlement.

"Isko, I have decided to sell our land to Mr. and Mrs. Monteverde. If it happens, I can only guess what they might plan to do with it but as new owners they can do with it in any way they wish."

"Does it really matter, Patricio? That's who they are but that's not what we are. People in the lowland now call our land as Hacienda Bartolome because of some paper that you produced but that's between them and you. It does not concern us. We are not part of it. That's how they think and it pains me that you think like them now. You know that this land belongs to no one and that our people have always enjoyed its fruits from the beginning of time. How can a piece of paper change all that?"

"You have to understand, Isko, that we now live in a different world, a different time and a different way of thinking. And so, we need to behave differently. It means that we have to adapt to newer ways of seeing and doing things."

"Like the fact that they can now tell us what to do and not to do? What gives them power over us and over our land? Is it our problem that their world has become so complicated they consider ours does not exist anymore? Can you explain away with a piece of paper everything our ancestors have

26

imparted in our land? It doesn't really matter. Go now Patricio."

Don Patricio took out from his shirt pocket the last bite of the betel nut quid and gnawed it on the way home, this time gnashing his teeth harder and tighter. His resolve was firm that until he reached his house he would not bother to look back at all, to be enthralled as ever before by the rising majesty of Sumagang and her little one as he walked away from the imposing beauty with a heavy heart.

CHAPTER 6

Minandro was all alone sitting on a coconut stump that Don Patricio cut a few days ago. He was carving the ends of a bamboo stick with a bolo.

"What's that?" asked Don Patricio upon entering the Bartolome's dooryard, across the highway.

"A bow."

"A bow?"

"Yes."

"Hmm, where's guy, your buddy?"

"In the backyard."

"You're fighting again?"

"Yeah."

"Did you have your breakfast yet? By the way, your mother was looking for you."

"We had papaya."

"What's the bow for, anyway?"

"For the boars."

"Boars?" Don Patricio didn't expect any answer and then he spat out the rubbish in his mouth before going to see his son.

He found Salvio carving his own bamboo stick.

"You're making a bow too?"

Salvio looked at his father and decided not to reply.

"Hey, I'm talking to you."

"You promised *Inay*³ not to go to the cockpit anymore. You always break your promise, *Itay*. I could see it in your face that you bet on the wrong cock again."

"No, I'm keeping my promise. I've just come from Minandro's house. I had a talk with Ymelda, your godmother."

"About my final grades, my place in the honors list? Itay, I had a hard time in fraction and —"

"No, we talked about something else. Trust me, *anak*. I'm not gambling again. Your *Manoy* Esteban needs the money to graduate. He's our only chance, your chance. I can't wager on that. Your Manoy, when he becomes a doctor, he will take care of Panchito's matriculation. Chito's going to graduate from law in two years. Yolanda wants to be in Manila too, and that's next year. She says only in her wildest dreams she'll

---

³ *Inay*: Mother; *Itay*: Father; *anak*: Son; *Manoy*: Title of respect for an elder brother

29

take up nursing in Ibana College, not when all her friends are planning to attend college in exclusive convent schools. So, I can't fool around anymore. Please trust me, cockfighting is over for me."

Don Patricio paused for a moment hoping his explanation was persuasive enough, and then went on to pry again into a puerile feud, "Well, anak, what's wrong with the two of you, are you fighting again?"

Salvio was still skeptical with his father's answer but he felt the need to be more responsive to the last question.

"Itay, Minandro is stubborn. He doesn't believe in what Inay and you told me about Sumagang. He doesn't believe in anything anymore, that giant animals live with giant trees, plants, mushrooms, weeds, vines, orchids, flowers and all those humungous weird creatures and vegetation. They'd all thrived in Sumagang at least before I was born or before you were born, hadn't they, Itay?

The old man tried to avoid the topic.

"Have you seen your cousin Efren? Your auntie has been looking for him since this morning."

"No. Efren always runs to his father in San Vicente whenever he has a fight with auntie. He'll be home in a day or two. But did you hear my question anyway?"

Don Patricio simply gave his son a blank look, a long empty look before going inside the house. Salvio wasn't sure whether the strangeness in his father's eyes meant there are still many things untold about Sumagang, or Minandro's obstinacy has better legs to stand on than the tales from his old folks that he has learned to venerate.

Pigheaded or not, Minandro has gained confidence and become a great shot following his first kill in the bamboo grove and since then he has started collecting the largest wing feather of every game bird he has killed hoping to display them one day in a frame in the boy's room. He was in fact sharper when using Salvio's favorite slingshot, the one with the perfect "Y" for a grip that Salvio had given him as one of those one-sided gestures of appeasement. While Minandro believed he was the better shot of the two of them, he had long conceded that Salvio had a natural gift for crafting the best wood handle for their weapons.

And now, he was sure Salvio was making the perfect bow and the perfect arrows again, and he needed Salvio to come over to him and share his expertise, to tell him why his bamboo was not curving right to make a balanced bow. But as usual Minandro was too proud to make the first move or too assured Salvio would soon come and show him exactly which part of the bamboo to thin off to make that perfect bend.

The peace offering was longer to come and Minandro, all wound up in frustration the next time he broke another bamboo stick, clobbered the coconut stump with the bolo repeatedly. The loud wallops were meant not so much to let his steam out as to call Salvio's attention.

Salvio was well aware the tantrums were going on in silence even before Minandro's distress calls were sounded. The last time Salvio had seen that temper was still vivid to him. They were in kadlagan and up on a balaigang tree when Minandro began singing *The Magic Touch.* Salvio always loved his guy crooning especially in a cappella, with only the stomping of a foot, the beating of a stick, or Minandro's own instrumental background and adlibs, the plaintive *oh uh ohs,* and the short and long *ah ahs* as accompaniments. You will win the amateur contest in Naga City, just try, Salvio would often prod his guy. But Minandro would be full of confidence only with his buddy as the audience. While Salvio has known Minandro as too public as a frog with his rage, he alone is privy to the sensibilities of a boy trying to reach out, share his warmth and tenderness or bare his very soul with his songs, whether the rendition, even in his pre-teen voice, was in Sinatra, Pat Boone, Perry Como, or Elvis Presley. Minandro unabashedly would gyrate, throw and swing his feet around and contort his lips when doing *Don't be Cruel, Poor Boy* or *Jail House Rock*, all in their private concert.

But, this time, Salvio could not stand the way Minandro was delivering *you oo o got.*

"Shouldn't it be *you-oo-'ve got?*" he finally interrupted. The one-man band abruptly stopped as if by the exact signal of the wand from a conductor in full control of an ensemble.

"If it's *you have got,* then you use *gotten,*" Minandro insisted, slowly emphasizing every syllable of his sentence.

"It's should be *you've got*, that's how Americans do it, or how Negroes say it. It was your mother who told our class it's an exception to the rule," Salvio refused to yield.

"It goes smoothly when you don't have the *'ve*," Minandro raised his voice.

"I'm sure it's *you've got*. Hundred percent sure," was the derisive answer.

"Sure, you're sure," Minandro yelled back, kicking the branch Salvio was perched on.

Salvio's fast reflexes by holding tight prevented him from being shaken off and falling 30 feet below. Obviously bothered by the pallid face of Salvio, Minandro scampered down like a frightened monkey, and headed into the woods, deep into the sanctuary of their kadlagan. They didn't speak to each other for three days after that tussle in proper American English. When Salvio initiated the peace move, he lost to Minandro his slingshot with the snake handle and the perfect "Y".

Salvio wanted not to give in yet, not until he tested his new handiwork. He pulled the string of the bow several times. This is just perfect, the young bowyer assured himself. Feeling ready, he proudly walked toward the front yard where his poor Minandro was still fuming. Minandro's eyes were fixed to the ground while his ears were wide open for any signs of succor, any solace, any of those all-too consoling approaches of someone who's always there when he couldn't handle himself.

The voice and the touch finally came.

"LB, try this one. The strength of the string is just right for you." There was a momentary pause. The Platters' lyrics became alive.

> *You-oo-'ve got the magic touch*
> *You make me glow so much*
> *It casts a spell, it rings a bell*
> *The magic touch*

Minandro carefully turned his stare from the ground to what struck him as a stunning workmanship by a 10-year old boy.

"Is—is this strong enough for wild boars?" he asked, while feeling the prized slingshot in his trousers' back pocket, to be sure it was still there.

"I guess so, guy. Why don't you try it with this arrow?"

The arrow, a Chinese bamboo the size of a pinkie, was taller than Salvio, the head artfully crowned with duck feathers for steadiness and the tip made of stainless metal forged out of a car wiper Salvio scoured from BITRANCO's junkyard. Minandro slowly let go of the bulge in his pocket, and reached in awe for the bow and the arrow in front of him.

"Guy HB, I think this is strong enough, yes even for giant boars," Minandro reassured his guy.

Salvio grinned ear to ear.

"That yours now guy LB, I'll make another one for me tomorrow."

CHAPTER 7

"Pa, do you know that the headless body they found on the highway was the Mayor's bodyguard's? Someone, a boy, discovered the dead man's head hanging from the *acacia* in front of the Central School, his mutilated genitals stuck in his mouth. The kid's probably a witness to the murder."

Leo, who already learned some details of the grisly news during the Sunday homily, eyeballed Antonio momentarily before side-glancing at Rebecca, warning his son in effect to use only appropriate language before the dinner table, and then he continued to nibble at the fried mudfish. His appetite belied his slim and muscular build. The coconut cooking oil coating his fingers and mouth matched those glazing his high forehead.

"This is the same guy who raped a mother and her 13-year old daughter in barrio San Pedro," Antonio pressed on to tell more of what he had earlier gathered from Coty's Store. "The *sari-sari* store was abuzz with terribly appalling details, do you know that?"

"Is Minandro still upstairs?" Leo asked, addressing no one, to change the conversation.

"No, pa, he's been with you know who since this morning," Rebecca promptly chimed in to let everyone know she had a part to play in the table talk.

"Someone's laid a wreath with a black ribbon at the Mayor's doorstep," Antonio stuck to his subject.

"Where did you get that one?" Leo, with that fresh scoop, finally reacted to his son.

"From the sari-sari store."

The normally prying Ymelda, seated at the other end of the table opposite Leo, looked so immersed in something else that a headless corpse for a mealtime piece seemed palatable at the moment. She also didn't notice that Rebecca has not touched her food or Minandro's seat was empty. She has worn that dumbfounded look since Don Patricio's visit.

"How can a handful of brigands terrorize a town of 100,000?" Antonio became more probing. "We speak freely against Mayor Magbanua, his acts and his politics, or the abuses of his brother Warlito but when the New Pilipino Army, the NPA, strikes, everyone is silenced. Even Mr. de la Rama, his notorious vociferousness notwithstanding, is practically tongue-tied. He was there when the gruesome grapevine reached the store yet he was so cautious to make any of his usual political wisecracks, his arrogant punditry. When they pressed him for an opinion, he turned grim, even ashen and then he left without saying a word. He made everyone feel that whatever you say—that the store is wired to the people on the other side of Sumagang."

That last word caught Mrs. Monteverde's attention.

"How much do you know about the people on the other side, Antonio?"

"In fact very little, ma. But in our History class, our teacher said that the government is refusing to acknowledge the seriousness of their presence in the area. One of my classmates claims their leader is a ruthless University of the Philippines guy. Pa is a UP graduate and he teaches in our school now and he always talks with *Tito*[4] Sal, the *commie* professor, you know, of Ibana College. They're perpetually engaged in some discourse, even during the homily. Maybe, Pa knows more."

Antonio was certainly baiting his father to open up and get engaged. Leo did but hesitantly.

"Isn't that what I was trying to explain to you this morning, Ymelda? Pading Patricio's offer to you about his iliyan property is exceedingly tempting but we could have some problems with these people on the other side. Some of our town mates in the know believe these people are merciless. Now, they can prove they are."

"That's plain nonsense, Leo." Mrs. Monteverde dropped her guard. "I still know most of the people on the other side

---

[4] *Tito*. Uncle or title of respect for an elder man

of the mountain. I used to be their head teacher and the only people I know in the foothills of Sumagang to be ruthless are none other than the bodyguards of the brother himself of Mayor Magbanua. The peasant boy they manhandled some years ago—was that Justino or Justo, he was one of my sixth-grade pupils—he became a paraplegic for a while and I guess he still couldn't walk."

"Ma, Justo is a bum. He was drunk and crossed the road without looking. Warlito avoided hitting him with his Honda and he ended up in the ditch. Good thing he had his helmet on. Look, Justo is only lame in the day but he can dance the Merengue with those *saloneras*[5] till the wee morning hours."

"That's not even the point, Antonio. It was an accident, nobody intended to hurt anyone when it all started. But Warlito Magbanua and his men took it upon themselves to mistreat Justo. The poor fellow was not even 13 years old then. What's worse, when Justo's father complained at the City Hall, they locked him up supposedly for smelling up the investigator's office with Ginebra or something. He's a very shy farmer, seldom in town, and he had to take a jigger or two, they said, to keep his mettle. Some hard core criminals he was mixed up with in the city jail assaulted him badly. It's just injustice on top of another."

"Should one get decapitated for such an injustice? I don't get that line, ma."

---

[5] *saloneras*: Dancing partners for a fee

"What makes you so sure this was the work of the people on the other side?"

"Ma, it's just how they do it. First, they summon their condemned by sending them a wreath with a black ribbon. Then, they proceed *ex parte* and *in absentia* before dispensing their own brand of justice, if you can call that justice at all."

"Do you think Judge Torda will dispense justice when it's Warlito who is on the deck? Torda is both spineless and lawless. That bar-flunker doesn't know the law, and if he does, he doesn't have the nerve to say what it is, to people like Warlito.

"Whose side are you on, ma?"

"And on whose side are you, Antonio?"

"Ma, I'm not rooting for any side or any ideology. I take on both sides of the issue. That's why the KMP in our school, an NPA front, if you don't know yet, has not been able to sign up a new member out of your son because while I listen I reason out. Justice is reason. A good reason gives way to a better reason. Fighting injustice with another injustice is like building a vessel riddled with holes."

"That sounds Confucian. O-or Leorian punditry? I wonder how it shapes up in college a month from now."

Leo ignored the swipe.

"More rice please," Rebecca yelled at the maids in the kitchen, her purpose was to hold down the rising tone of the conversation. "What's punditry, is that bad?" Rebecca spoke directly to her father to get him into the act but he was too busy finishing up his second mudfish.

"You mean banditry, Rebecca," Antonio rebuffed and blamed his little sister for being thrown off. "Ask Mr. Webster."

"I'm not even seven years old."

"Pundit is to punditry and bandit is to banditry," the pedagogue was obliged to explain the way she would to her fourth-grade class.

"What's a pundit?

"Well, a pundit is—is like your papa, passionate only when talking with another know-it-all bighead. Otherwise, he would rather wrestle with fish heads." It was Ymelda's cruel way to spite Leo for brushing off the repeated invitations to intellectualize the exchange.

"Pundit sounds like Chinese food, he he." Rebecca's peculiar giggle always lightens up her father. But *pansit* noodle and *estopado* were what Leo thought would be dinner that tonight.

"Speak of the devil, I hear Kiong Fu coming," Leo smirked after saying that last one. His intent was to make amends but the attempt at good humor was ill-timed at best.

Minandro first hid his stuff, his bow and arrow behind the santol tree before going inside the house. He pretty much knew what's coming to him.

Ymelda flicked a slap at his cheek when the son attempted to greet the mother with a kiss. "Minandro, I want you to wash up right now and go to bed. No dinner," Mrs.

Monteverde gave him no chance at all to hold her in any argument. So far, she had enough of it.

"This is not the first time you were late for dinner this week."

Ignoring everyone around the dining table and whatever food was on it, Minandro repaired directly to the kitchen door leading out to the backyard, fetched a pale of water from the deep well, washed his feet and went inside again to ask for his father's blessings for the evening. When he kissed the back of his father's hand with his forehead, he felt the heavy grease from the fried mudfish. Rebecca saw Minandro smirked—the Monteverde way, and thought something was fishy.

The boys' room is elevated by a couple of feet from the floorboard of the upper floor and except for the entrance from the veranda, it is separated from the bedrooms and the family room by a solid wooden wall. An undersized door and a staircase as narrow as a portable ladder connect the room to the veranda. The mini side window of the room frames the peak of Sumagang and one looking through the front window would feel like surveilling the front yard and the national highway from a watch tower.

The bed Minandro shared with his brother was half-empty that night. Antonio had to take on Minandro's role to be with Rebecca to play outside. It was third-quarter moon and the children had not gotten over yet the summer fever. The highway was their playground. The field of play was lined by watermarks, the water drawn from the Monteverde deep well time and again as it evaporates easily in the summer even in the evening. The rules of the game were simple but they always had great fun.

Minandro refused to look through the window, preferring to lie down to appreciate the mystique of Sumagang in the moonlight vitiated intermittently by the silhouettes of flying bats. Whenever the collective laughter could not drown the high-pitched shriek of Salvio, Minandro could not help but smile. It was past curfew time when Rebecca went to bed and Antonio did not notice his bedmate pretending to be asleep.

Certain that his brother was soundly snoozing, Minandro went down the staircase at way past midnight, and tiptoed on the veranda toward the main stairway and down to the living room. Downstairs, Minandro cautiously opened the narra door by lifting it a bit to avoid the screeching sound it usually creates, and then he walked up to the santol tree to pick a bundle he had hanged there. He peeled off the layer of smoked banana leaves wrapping. Minandro smiled ear to ear. In it was, well, a late dinner, a mound of brown rice topped by a huge fried mudfish. Salvio prepared it for dear guy LB.

CHAPTER 8

If dilettante photographers prefer to shoot a broad vista of the town against Sumagang from the church belfry, a true artist will capture the beauty of the mountain on a canvas easeled in the heart of the Ibana College campus. Between the open athletic field of the College and Sumagang is an exhilarating rolling plain broken up only by a couple of *nipa* huts dotting the rice meadow on the fringe of the campus ground and by the spattered rooftops of houses on the far horizon leading to the foothills. The Monteverde residence is one of those houses but from the campus, it is too minute to be recognized by anyone or trivial enough it could be easily brushed off into the green cover by a careless stroke.

For the past decade or so, Mr. Leo Monteverde has taken his routine stroll around the track and field oval after his classes, or during break, but he actually has not encountered any artist painting the scenery on a canvas. The College, for one thing, offered no course in Fine Arts and therefore there were no students who would spend the day out in the field working on art projects. A career in arts was uppity in Y-riga (the few who thought they were potential maestros would consider it a sin to be a product of a provincial college) or a waste of time (there's not a single art shop in town and the only artist that's known made his living only during elections producing political streamers on silk screens). Churning out nurses, midwives and nannies for export has so far made the school, the community, and everyone come out as winners in the economic scheme of things.

Who else could be held in awe by an ancient grandeur but a handful of strangers, visitors or new students from far away regions? For quite a time, Mr. Monteverde himself has not conversed with Sumagang even in his rare lyrical mood. Lately, he has drawn inspirations from other subjects for his poetry. The last one was a failed attempt at a modernist form about the brothel across the school, and he tried other unfamiliar themes too. It just seemed that familiarity has a harsh way of making people insensitive to many things they otherwise value dearly, until their possessions of those things are challenged. The thought suddenly struck Mr. Monteverde.

In fact there were many more things going on inside Mr. Monteverde when he started his walk. He felt he was losing his hold of the Ymelda he had known for many years. She has increasingly grown ambivalent. Her intense interest in acquiring landholdings was transforming her in ways that ran recklessly at crosscurrents with some unwelcome incidents on the other side of the mountain. The growing incidence of *kaingin* on Sumagang has highlighted the changes Mr. Monteverde has noticed in his spouse. Typically, when the smell of brush fires was strong enough to reach the lowlands, Ymelda would raise hell—although only before the venue of their dining table. Mr. Monteverde was also missing her familiar tirade against BITRANCO for regularly dumping used engine oil into the creek that runs from the mountain through the stream forming the once pristine brookside. The family knew there was too much complicity in illegal logging involving high-placed local and military officials and private cohorts, and Ymelda has persistently ranted about it if only as a reminder of the pitfall of social irrelevance if issues of those sorts were ignored. For the impressionable Minandro, it was a family routine that has helped engrain in him a peculiar reverence for Sumagang. But of late, her diatribes have waned. *Whose side my wife is on now?* Antonio's question the last time resonated anew.

Mr. Monteverde noticed the sun about to set and hide behind the modern multi-story building of Ibana College. The track would soon be lighted. The professor-writer was nevertheless feeling good in his new reflections, about coming back to something old. And as he turned again facing the mountain for the next lap, Mr. Monteverde couldn't help but be transfixed by the commanding heights in front of him. He hadn't had that experience for a while.

"You're too early for the next race, Sal," Mr. Monteverde teased his colleague who was putting on his Converse shoes on the side of the track.

"I was tied up with Ed, Edgardo you know." Professor Salvador Palma tried to apologize as his walking partner slowed down to stop. "Move on, I'll catch up with you, Leo."

While still reflective in his subconscious, Mr. Monteverde got excited somehow and figured he'd get more juicy news about the headless body and the missing boy witness. Ed was an aboveground KMP member who liked to confide in Mr. Palma.

The latecomer waited for his partner to complete the turn before starting his laps, and then the two walked together at a quickened pace, as if by doing so their conversation would be more private, more secure.

"These are ominous times," Mr. Leo Monteverde narrowed the time-frame and the topic of the conversation right away.

"It depends." Mr. Palma was illusive. "It depends upon what context you are coming from."

"There's only one. And that's the rule of law."

"You're either pretending to be naïve or too legalistic. It's just payback time. Can't you trim it down that way?"

"Do you want this town to be brutish and nasty?"

"Enough of Hobbesian talk, Professor Leo. It's always been an eye for an eye, a tooth for a tooth. Any deviation from that is sheer capriciousness of the lawgiver. Look, *padre,*[6] it is one thing to have a system and be made to believe in its pretenses. It's another when those who have the means take it upon themselves to read the mandates one way or the other all for their own sake. The rest gets a raw deal. Well, what's in the name, if the will is there, anything works."

"How could you entrust the future of your family in a guy like Edgardo? Be real, Sal. What does he know about running the lives of 40 million Filipinos?"

"Ed or his kind is a pawn, you know that, just as we were pawns of the GIs. Of course, he won't run the show. This UP kid, this smart guy from Diliman—this much I heard of him. He is ready to fight ideas with ideas. His way is to let the many see their power, then, turn the Empire against its footmen, the footmen against the Empire, and the Empire against itself. He's aware that nationalism and patriotism satisfy a psychological need for national identity and pride, but to him there's a greater need for self-respect that transcends tribalism and parochialism. His messianic message is supposed to rescue not only our small island but all who are oppressed, poor, and weak. It is supra-political. He's not only a good shepherd, a scholar of their law but also lives it."

"Interesting, very interesting, Sal. And now that you've gone full circle, don't you agree that ultimately wherever you

---

[6] *padre:* Short for compadre

47

go it's a matter of rule of law?" Leo attempted to take a higher ground.

"Define that for me," Mr. Palma, his voice rising, taunted his compadre.

"There's got to be some rules somewhere that we can concur on because the alternative is just plain folly." Leo remained calm yet unyielding.

"Now, you're going full circle yourself around those myths. Rules somewhere? Justice precedes rule. Get that one, please. Alright, Leo, who sets the rules now? I don't, you don't. We are all on the receiving end. The rule is as well-entrenched as that ancient monster, that mountain up there. It can only be uprooted with a new system of rules or by its own implosion. And even if it occurs, it won't fizzle out like a bad dream. It will continue to haunt us as it lurks there as real as a phantom from eons ago. Isn't that *simple* enough?"

"Simple? Simplistic, maybe. But the world, this town is not as simple as a pleasure walk on this manicured turf of the campus or—"

"Look, we made the rules during our guerilla days, didn't we?" Mr. Palma cut off his colleague. And then his disposition transformed. "We believed we were serving a just cause when we mutilated those Japanese collaborators the same way we had tortured house lizards in our cruel child play. We torched and buried alive those whom we judged to be traitors in the secret crevasses of Sumagang. Just look straight out there. Doesn't it remind us that we were once the law?"

No one talked during the next lap. It was a long walk, a much longer and painful walk. For humiliating his friend and himself, Mr. Palma was so discomfited how he wished he could scamper astray from the oval track like a child in fright. On his part, Mr. Monteverde imagined the lanes actually straightened up toward the school gate, out to the crowded streets of the town where he hoped to be lost. But there was no dignified way to avoid the turn and confront their tormentor eyeball to eyeball. Sumagang would not tire waiting in watchful eye and the most elementary honor demanded they must make the full circle.

CHAPTER 9

"In the mountain of the Lord's temptation, Jesus rejected the Devil's bribery with political power; on the last mountain, the Lord called out his Apostles to service, to 'make disciples of all the nations'; and in the mountains in between, the Lord taught and cured." Father Barrameda began his Palm Sunday homily with a bang. "The meek shall inherit the earth, so 'put your sword into its scabbard.'" The firm voice from the pulpit of the handsome 31-year old priest reached an early crescendo and reverberated in the church to the silent consternation of Monsignor who was listening behind the altar. "Didn't Jesus, a male, a Jew, a rabbi, acknowledge in public, in a serious spiritual exchange, a nameless woman, a Samaritan, a despised underclass? Didn't the Son of Man in his own peculiar way rebelled against man's law by refusing to use power as the best way to exercise that selfsame power?"

"Whose side is he on?" Mr. Palma asked.

Leo did not answer and remained standing by the church doorway, deeply contemplative. Mr. Palma himself decided to stay put. Antonio ignored the usual movement of his crew to step outside during the homily and congregate in the patio as he kept his attention to the pulpit while closely watching the body language of his father and Mr. Palma. Salvio fidgeted on a pew in the middle of the church and began to ponder whether the plan to climb iliyan leaked out. The poor kid looked around the church for some clue but only the absence of guilt on Minandro's face assuaged him. On the other hand, the assembly was waiting patiently for any reference in the homily about the headless body on the highway.

The normally affable Mayor Magbanua was uncharacteristically serious while seated on the first row, and listened motionless to the homily. From the vantage of the elevated pulpit, Father Barrameda saw Mr. Palma, Leo and Antonio conspicuously remaining standing by the church's main doorway. Lurking at the far end of the right wing of the church was Edgardo, the student leader, whose searching eyes, like those of some anxious parishioners, were as much trained towards Mayor Magbanua as to the preacher. The mayor was visibly trying hard to catch the eye of the young priest, ready to communicate his displeasure should the preaching go overboard. And every time certain lines of the sermon in English were repeated in the Y-riga dialect, the interest of the congregation intensified. Rebecca herself was a bit bemused as she observed her mother take unusual curiosity in the homily and stop praying the rosary.

Smart enough not to meet headlong the silent bullying of Mayor Magbanua, Father Barrameda avoided eye contact with the people on the front seats and yet kept his audience engaged even as he sounded both unyielding and farfetched: "When the Lord said 'You shall love your neighbor as your self,' he meant it *now*! For service to the poor in the hereafter is not man's realm. Activism is not allowed in heaven. We all know that, don't we? Love, our neighbor, and justice for the poor make 'rational' selfishness unspiritual. We simply cannot be Christian in isolation. Christian or not, no man is an island. We must find Christ in the service of others, in the freedom and human dignity in others. The world cannot be any better if we look first and foremost to our self-interest. Jesus, our Lord, did not deny the poor their heaven on earth. Justice until Judgment Day is Mary-come-lately." That last line halted the steady march of Mrs. Marie Alvarez along the center aisle. More confused than mortified, she was forced to take a seat in between Salvio and Minandro.

It was the very first time Minandro has been so up-close to one of the town's matrons. As Mrs. Alvarez settled on the pew, her hemline shrunk a few more inches from her knees exposing the naked whiteness of her thighs not covered by the fancy stockings. Minandro nervously examined her foot-to-head. His side-glances lingered a bit more on the cleavage of her breasts and then he let his curiosity dawdled upon her glossy lips, the thickly reddened cheeks and fake eyelashes. Inching even closer to sniff her perfume, Minandro found out, to his chagrin, the matron didn't have the pleasant herbal smell of his mother. But the not-so-motherly Mrs. Alvarez looked much like those sexy models on the ads of the *Journal of Education*.

"Infierno!" Father Barameda thundered from the pulpit. Minandro woke up from his arousal and embarrassed himself as he saw Salvio winking desperately at him.

"Everyone has his or her own Calvary to bear. Sometimes we do it for ourselves. At other times we do it for others. The goals and consequences of our actions are multifarious: from sharing pain to wallowing in pleasure, from short-term profit to lasting perdition. As you leave this church to continue the celebration of our Lord's triumphant entry into our lives, we should pray and hope to be taught and be cured in the mountains we choose to climb."

"Oh my—how could you do this to me, Minandro," Salvio finally let out his suspicion.

CHAPTER 10

Before going to bed, Salvio was anxious reviewing his checklist for the mountain climb. He learned how to do the simple planner from Mrs. Monteverde's science class. The system came in handy once during a Boy Scout camping two summers ago.

The list written on a piece of lined yellow paper apparently went in an order of priorities:

1. Slingshot
2. 20 round pebbles (from brookside)
3. Uncle Fred's army belt
4. Canteen
5. Binoculars
6. Rope and string
7. At least 5 strips of Band-Aid, and
8. Rubbing alcohol.

No sooner had Salvio lied flat on his back than he began to transport himself to an imagined realm, somewhere in the midst of a thicket where the bushes are oversized and the creatures that abound acting up like humans. But the wild make-believe, a routine amusement for him, produced goose bumps this time. He decided not to immerse in his imaginings; instead, he tried to while away what has become to be a long night by recalling a funny campout incident, about one Boy Scout camper who relied entirely on his senile grandmother to pack his things. The infantile lout had to contend with a guava twig, beaten on one end, to serve as his toothbrush for the duration of the three-day camporee. Another boy, Salvio's tent-mate, brought only one pair of socks which he wore round the clock— and Salvio was sure the sloth has never taken a shower since day one of the camping. The putrid odor the socks generated inside the unventilated tent stuck to Salvio's olfactory nerves days after the outing. Those losers!

Still restless, Salvio again shifted his thoughts—away from the fantasyland of giant vegetations.

Well, was Minandro only pulling my leg when he denied any complicity?

He decided not to find any answer anymore how Father Barrameda supposedly found their covert plan. Until he fell asleep, he had been debating whether he would also bring his uncle's 20-inch Japanese bayonet.

What will Minandro say if I do? He listed it as the 9th item; then crossed it out again.

For days since the plan for the trek was finalized at the belfry, Salvio has began studying the timing of the morning roosters crowing from their backyard. The first to break the pre-dawn silence was almost always singular, probably from the same bird, then, in interval of no more than a minute, followed by another, and yet another. That's around three o'clock in the morning, Salvio has figured it out, because that's when he also would hear the first BITRANCO bus to hit the highway for "the early birds," those merchants with their wares to ply in Naga, the Big City of the Bikol region, and with whom the family traveled in the same trip schedule during the last Lady of *Peñafrancia* pilgrimage.

In the next hour, the second bout of riser shrills would be a chorus of at least five roosters in quick and urgent alternating wake-up calls as if issued by an eager drill sergeant to his platoon for the early morning run. Salvio also noted the church bells were sounded for the daily churchgoers past four o'clock. We should hit the ground by then—before Auntie Pinay rises to prepare the rice coffee, he calculated.

I will bring my hunting knife tomorrow, Minandro made up his mind in the quiet of the boys' room. But his thoughts were interrupted. A lizard crawling on the ceiling snapped an unsuspecting insect. That triggered the legends surrounding

Sumagang suddenly unraveling on the blank surface like a science fiction or horror thriller, sending chills down Minandro's spine. Alone in the room, he was spooked, wishing he were beside mom, holding her ears to lull him to sleep as he had been used to as a little one. The tale among the *gurang*[7] was first to come live on the imagined screen.

Some town elders still treat the mountains of Bikol region as super beings, and the folklore goes that Mt. Mayon, still a very active volcano today, attempted to steal the unborn iliyan by forcing open the belly of Sumagang. Mt. Isarog came to rescue Sumagang and aborted the violent abduction by impaling Mayon's head with a lance. Mayon managed to escape but abandoned iliyan to die by the wayside in the wake of the violence. Sumagang expired too almost instantly and did not witness the heroic feat of Isarog whose wounds borne during the struggle proved to be similarly fatal. Mayon, on the other hand, survived its injury but the grave wrong it committed angered the Gods so much so it was decided the one wound the condemned wrongdoer sustained would never heal in order that it would continually suffer from smoldering hemorrhage till the end of time.

It's the version of Don Patricio explaining the chasmal scar of Sumagang that Minandro found more convincing. He refused to play it back in his mind that night. According to that story retold to him by Salvio at the belfry, the behemoths of the ancient have taken refuge in Sumagang to escape the

---

[7] *gurang*: Older folks

big floods but never returned to the lowlands even after the waters had receded; when the growth of the mammoths' population in the belly of the Sumagang became unsustainable, their habitat caved in burying every giant reptiles alive.

The little house reptile on the ceiling came crashing to the floor before getting the chance to digest its catch. It was separated from its tail on being blasted by a paper ball Minandro flung from his slingshot. Minandro missed the target again with his second shot as the tailless creature scampered outside through the side window.

"What was that?" Mrs. Monteverde yelled from the adjacent room.

"I dropped my book."

"Is Antonio back yet?"

"No."

For a moment Minandro thought he saw the phantom of the lizard fade into the wilderness and wrote it off as a fallen beast. Now, from his bed he fixed his stare past iliyan, at the splendor of Sumangang cased by the boys' room's window. The mountain looked closer to him than it presented itself that night. Between them the strange nocturnal mood was mutual, almost communicative. Yet he resolved: I'll bring my knife. I won't let Salvio know.

Minandro spotted a fleck of light from the depths of one slope of the mountain; the distant flicker could be easily mistaken as just another of the fireflies milling about the santol crown right outside where the lizard could have flown off for safety. *Santilmo?* He drew his knife to his side. Santilmos are ghostly fireballs often seen on the horizons believed by townsfolk to represent the spirit of someone who has either committed suicide or has been murdered. If they appear at sea, they spell disaster for seamen. If seen on land, they lead people to roam astray.

Minandro stiffened up. Nah, the kaingeros are at it again—they never learn. This time, he reached for the bow and arrows under his bed to make sure the weapons were still there. Maybe the Agtas had a late catch and they are just roasting it just now.

The bonfire was coming from a lair deep down the enormous declivity Sumagang is famous for—a gaping scar of difficult childbirth left open in its bosom, the favored lore townspeople often impress visitors with. The widest span of the deep crevasse is about a quarter of a mile from the ridgeline of one side to the other. That's what's visible. The legends surrounding Sumagang's wound are just conflicting.

CHAPTER 11

Huddled around a campfire on a clearing in the inmost jungle of Sumagang were five barefoot guerillas cuddling their M16s as they squatted on the dirt. Behind them was a makeshift palm hut. Inside the hut and in fetal curl on one end was a boy sobbing intermittently, his eyes already swollen, his right plastic flip-flops ostensibly missing. Across was another shelter, and standing by the window partly hidden by an overgrown fern was the figure of another guerilla in pensive mood. A wind shift brushed his cover aside allowing the campfire's flame to intrude his quite, exposing his handsome features. He was possibly in early thirties, about five feet ten inches tall and medium-built. The black Elpo rubber shoes he was wearing matched the badly beat-up fatigue shorts. His shirt and the .45 caliber pistol dangling from his waist were army issues. As the men outside noticed his presence, he stepped down from the shed and walked past them, patting one on the shoulder without saying a word. He stooped down in front of the hut and asked permission to crawl in. The boy inside responded only with two successive sobs, just somewhat louder this time.

"So you're Efren," he spoke gently as he kneeled on the ground. "Have you eaten your *camote*[8]? Sorry, that's what we have for the day. Tomorrow, we'll have better food. There will be a celebration."

The boy ignored him.

"Call me Kuya Dilim and don't be afraid, you'll be fine if you behave."

Still no answer but sobs.

"Who is your mother?"

"Inay must be very worried now," Efren finally uttered something. "You have to let me go. I'm not going to tell anyone, just let me go."

"You do know why you are here. If you want us to believe you then tell us what you saw."

"I saw men ganging up on another. I know no one of them. I hid in the bush because I was afraid. I closed my eyes when one screamed in great pain. That's all. Please let me go home to Inay, please." His eyes, pleading more desperately than his words, seemed to have struck a chord.

"Sleep now." The tone was a bit soothing. "Let's talk some time tomorrow. Eat your camote."

---

[8] *camote*: Yam

After a brief silence, the sobbing became inaudible but plaintive.

He stood up and cued the guerillas outside to follow him.

"All of us Kumander?"

"No, one of you please stay behind, watch the kid. And put out the fire thoroughly."

During the short walk deeper into the woods, the image of Efren, or specifically the boy's peculiar side glance, took the hardened revolutionary back to poignant thoughts about his own son, Elmer, who could be of the same age by now as his hostage. Elmer now lived with his mom in a Manila suburb. When dad had abandoned his family and gone underground, mom was forced to allow herself and her son to be housed by her former boyfriend, a Manila detective. The guerilla leader resurfaced one night when news reached him through the rebel grapevine in the city that the officer sometimes mistreated his son. He barged into the detective's apartment in the dead of the night and shook him up, warning he would rip the man's heart out of his chest if he lay on Elmer ever again.

Diliman's squad soon joined a larger platoon in the middle of a meal. The food consisted of boiled camote mashed with grated young coconut. Kumander Diliman greeted a youthful guerilla strumming a guitar and humming what sounded to be a patriotic song. The latecomers respectfully squeezed themselves into the group and settled down in the grass to partake of the supper but their leader who strode further towards the platoon's armory. He was followed by a woman guerilla and two other men who rose up. All four repaired to one end of the armory which included M16s, carbines, AK 47s, grenade launchers and WWII mortars. They began to engage in a hushed conversation.

"Our Edgardo is a goner if we allow the kid to go home." The warning given by Leila was grim. "They get Edgardo, they get every KMP in Ibana College. If not the military, that monster Warlito will bury each of our guys alive." The tone was unsympathetic, leaving no trace of the dainty former inter-collegiate beauty queen that Leila had once been.

"But what's in the book"? There's a bit of wiliness in the rhetorical question posed by Jacob almost nonchalantly. The defrocked catholic priest meant it to concur with the points Leila raised.

Rudy, the youngest among the committee of four, might have sealed the fate of the boy held hostage with a plain conspiratorial appeal to elementary dogma. "The communal interest is paramount." For his age, Rudy was eerily cold-blooded: "We cannot hold it in further abeyance. Efren must go."

"Go where?" Somewhat confused, Diliman sought clarification, looking each one directly in the eyes.

"For the higher purpose of the collective, we need to get rid of Efren when we get rid of the two kaingeros we captured. Summarily, that is."

CHAPTER 12

Kumander Diliman was not the only one in torment that night. Back in the Monteverde residence, Leo was wide awake, just as was his son Minandro in the boys' room, agonizing over the fate of his student Edgardo.

Edgardo, the son of a GI who opted to stay in the Philippines after marrying his mom, was a popular Ibana College campus figure especially among the coeds if only for his amber eyes. He was however also a former editor of the school paper and once a regional champion high school speller. His fervent wish had been to study in Manila at the National Science High School and then pursue a journalism degree at UP. But the veterans benefits Edgardo's father was receiving and the income the former US marine also earned from moonlighting as a test-driver at BITRANCO were not even enough to support his cockfighting and alcohol vices. To complement the family income, Edgardo's mother, a published poet, dabbled in dressmaking. Edgardo was 13 years old when his father succumbed to tuberculosis. It was during the same period his mother received a copy of a decision from a US court of appeals ruling as deserters a certain class of WWII soldiers that Edgardo's father was held to belong to. As a result, mother and son had to depend for sustenance on a monthly stipend of $75.00 from the generosity of Edgardo's maternal half-brother, a US Navy enlisted man.

Mr. Monteverde recalled Edgardo had been unusually active that day in his afternoon Political Science class. The professor spotted him flash a handsome grin on seeing the warm-up question written across the green board in all caps: CAN YOU FIND THE 'STATE' IN YOUR POCKET? The rest of his classmates, all ten of them, once inside the room looked at each other in silent fury, which went off almost in chorus that that's not what they had burnt their midnight candle for. Then Professor Leo began playfully to shuffle the class cards a few times, and each time the students felt their teacher was playing a Russian roulette for the dreaded graded recitation.

"So, Martin," the teacher gestured with his finger asking the first student called to rise, "is it there, in your pocket?"

"Of course not, sir," the student confidently answered as he was rising. "The state is also the government and the whole government cannot possibly fit in my pocket."

"In terms of size, which is where you want to take this class exercise to, it seems, do you think the state is bigger than the government?"

"Yes, of course. Aside from, aside from government, the state is also made up of people and its territory."

"If we take it that I'm the government in this room representing the sovereign state since I can basically command you to stand up or to sit down at will, free from external interference, and we have a definite territory, inhabited by eleven citizens, do you agree that we have just reduced a state to the size of a room—the size of Room E-203?

"Maybe, sir." The student's confidence began to erode.

"And if I can squeeze all eleven of you in my trousers' pocket, then it is possible to find a state in a pocket, is it not?"

The professor did not expect an answer, and after scribbling the grade on Martin's class card, he pulled the next one from the stack. "Is that right, hmm, Ed—gar—dooo?"

Edgargo made no hesitation. "Sir, the state is a state of mind. It is there or anywhere because we believe it. If we don't then it cannot exist. Belief in the existence of the state is like belief in the existence of a Supreme Being—or a god. The state is sovereign or God divine only if we allow it to be. You see, today, by the Jeffersonian *wall of separation*, we also revere that flag framed on the wall; yesterday, our ancestors thought everything depended on the whims of—the mountain out there. If you pronounced yourself as our supreme governor, sir, and that you or your realm, say Room E-203, and the state are one and the same, and all eleven of us believe, and consent to, those pronouncements, then so be it, Republic E-203 ours is."

"Say it differently."

"Well, differently put, the collective thought that today inspires our obeisance to our statehood and unites us behind it equates to the same mental and emotional state that allowed our forebears to worship the mountains—or consecrate the inviolability of nature."

The demeanor of Mr. Monteverde, who was impassive throughout Edgardo's rather fluid monologue, kept the class guessing whether the student activist had made a fool or a smart aleck of himself. The professor even turned quizzical to himself as soon as Edgardo had first completed his opening line. He was attentive to the philosophizing young man's chances of foundering on the rocks of *shallow draughts* while willing, on the other hand, to reconsider whatever impression he has had of the same truant student who barely made a passing grade in Philosophy the semester last.

And how has Mr. Palma gotten sold too on the grand of ideas of Kumander Diliman? The professor was in search for linkages.

Teach-ins? How often are these happening in the campus?

Meanwhile, slouched on his seat almost cockily after his discourse, Edgardo felt assured that the trick this time was on the middle-aged highbrow in front of him.

The animated class discussion—as well as the ongoing introspections—was rudely interrupted when a burly male barged into the classroom and accosted the teacher in front of the class. Three others were waiting outside. They were Warlito's henchmen. Edgardo's haughtiness quickly evaporated. He sat up haltingly and grew pale as he heard the intruder asked for him. Sensing grave danger, he begged his teacher not to let the men take him. Another went inside the room, warning the professor not to get involved. And when Edgardo tried to plead again, the man smacked Edgardo's face with a John Dewey hardcover he picked up from the teacher's desk, while the other guy physically restrained the professor for attempting to prevent the second strike. The murder instinct of the former guerilla fighter descended on the otherwise good-natured professor. But, his abstemious side prevailed, somehow, preventing him from doing anything stupid. The commotion invited the attention of two school security guards who were patrolling the hallway. The guards however walked past Room E-203 upon recognizing who were causing the trouble. The rest of the students remained still in their seats as they watched their classmate, bleeding from his nose and mouth, lifted from his feet and carried off by the four thugs outside the classroom and into a waiting jeep. The vehicle bore an official plate number.

Even as the entire class tried reconstituting itself from the shock during the remaining time before dismissal, Mr. Monteverde was on another plane extricating himself from a daemon of yesteryear that recurred to haunt him. The dormant trauma, or the tormented recall of role-reversal, mortified him more than the present. In the conjured images from the past, Captain Salvador Palma and Lieutenant Leo Monteverde and their men of the Kanlaon Guerilla Unit had been on the side of power; the hunted, a collaborator suspect, powerless and defenseless on his fateful day. Just as Warlito's goons, so also had the guerillas carried off their victim albeit in a more dramatic way. The poor fellow was inside the church when abducted—on his wedding day. He never made it to the altar to exchange vows with his bride.

Before the bell rang, Mr. Monteverde had managed to crack a cruel joke to the class. "The republic was short-lived."

CHAPTER 13

Rather than a wakeup call, the private turkey calls emanating from the kalachuchis turned out to be a come-out-now-and-let's-go call.

That's HB now.

Minandro lost no time collecting his school bag and the bow and arrows under his bed and rushed tiptoeing out of the boys' room and down the staircase. Because of the excitement, it escaped him altogether to lift the narra door before swinging it open. The creaking produced alerted his father still wrapped in deep introspection.

"Is that you, Antonio?"

"Uhmm."

"Don't forget to lock the door."

"Uhmm."

So, Minandro walked up the stairs again, slammed the boys' room door a bit and tiptoed downstairs the second time. He gently shut the main door of the house behind him as

Salvio nervously watched from under the shadow of the kalachuchis cast by the BITRANCO lamppost across the highway. Before setting out, Minandro picked some low-lying chicos and *balimbing*[9] from the garden and stuffed them into his backpack.

"That was close," Minandro expressed his relief as he approached the grinning Salvio at the gate.

"Did you bring the flag?"

Oh my, ah yes! I'll—I'll be right back."

And Minandro dashed back to the house and sneaked into the boys' room again, in perfect cadenced and coordinated fashion this time. He reached for his blanket, gathered it to his chest, then tiptoed down the staircase the third time. Finally, when he retuned to Salvio still patiently waiting at the property entrance, and still grinning, there was a mixed bag of exasperation and triumph visible in his face. It's one of those vulnerable moments that Salvio would find in Minandro his dear LB.

"I have no more room in my school bag, HB." Minandro seemed anxious yet.

"No sweat, guy LB. Give the blanket to me. I brought uncle's knapsack."

At five o'clock on a Holy Wednesday morning, dawn began breaking over the crest of Sumagang to soon blaze *Bocawe*, the main trail leading to the foothills of the

---

[9] *balimbing*: Starfruit

mountain. The trail actually commences as the dirt road splits towards east from the asphalted national highway after a row of three Spanish-era houses from the BITRANCO compound. On the left corner of the road, stands the 18th century old San Nicolas chapel securely separated from the highway by four huge boulders that are believed to be remnants of Sumagang's last fury. That morning, a couple of barrio faithfuls rose early to finish priming the elevated platform on the chapel yard to get it ready for the *Pasyon*. The structure had been constructed and donated to the barrio by an old-time resident. It was meant to be multi-purpose but, for the most part, it's been used as a convenient venue for varied political activities except, of course, during the Holy Week.

"Too early yet for the hunt," one of the guys working on the platform teased the two boys who started to pound on the dirt road. He obviously noticed the bow and arrows Salvio and Minandro were each carrying that outsized them.

"Hey, Nandro, is that you? does Ma'am Monteverde know where you guys are going? Don't get in trouble now, big guys," another worker continued the taunt.

"Careful brave hunters, mountain goblins are in their baddest during the Holy Week, ho ho ho," a third guy hooted.

The boys simply ignored the teasing and moved on to trek ahead. Salvio sensed something when Minandro tried to feel the hunting knife and slingshot inside his bag.

"Don't worry LB, Itay knows those guys, they're from *Kalye Supot.* They won't tell."

"How come your parents don't seem to mind at all whether you spend the whole day in kadlagan, in brookside, in the movie house, or anywhere?"

"Your father doesn't mind you too."

"No, I'm talking about my mother. Everything has to be done by the rules, her rules."

"Because she's a teacher and teachers have to go by the rules. That's what they are teachers for."

"I just think she cares more about Antonio than me. I don't even mind if she loves Rebecca more. Rebecca's still a baby."

"But Ma'am Monteverde talked as much about you as Antonio in our class. She even said once you are more like her as Antonio your dad."

"Anyway, if my mother finds out about the blanket I'll be in real big shit."

"But I thought you'd bring the maid's old blanket, not yours."

"Well, I actually forgot all about it, so I got my own blanket instead."

"Oh well, let's not just put up our flag anymore, so you could bring back home your blanket."

"Anyway, does anyone in your house know we are climbing iliyan?"

"Auntie Pinay knows. She always wants me to let her know whenever I go to far places. Although she wants me to tell cousin Efren to come home already, because she's no longer mad, if we happen to see him around."

About halfway through the mile-long walk, the two boys hopped over the ditch to allow the passing of a jeep ascending Bocawe in apparent haste which swerved towards them while struggling to negotiate the rock-strewn and potholed road. It left behind a cloud of dirt that lingered for a while. Minandro thought one of the passengers in the vehicle was familiar to him—or the jacket he was wearing. No sooner they returned to the middle of the street than two carabao-drawn carts travelling in tandem from the opposite direction forced them back to the ditch again as one of the riders, as youthful as Salvio, appeared to have lost control of the beast of burden. Two neighborhood dogs briefly chased the carts. The barking of the dogs and the exclamations from the street alerted some folks who had already risen for the day but none minded to investigate. One eyewitness looking out from the window of his hut, his elbows indolently rested on the bamboo frame while sipping rice coffee, exhibited little concern too. A younger fellow tending a tomato garden on the ground recognized Minandro.

"Hey, Minandro," the kid yelled out, waving a stick. Minandro recognized him and waved back.

"Who's that?" The man inside the hut asked after slurping down the last drop of the rice coffee.

"Ma'am Monteverde's son, Itay."

The traffic was quite atypical on Bocawe that morning especially on a Holy Week. At other times, the dirt road would be forlorn, trodden only by the indigenous Agtas who occasionally descend to the town proper and on normal days by the people whose shacks, few and far between, speckled the wooded roadsides. Most of the houses belong to the families of BITRANCO workers from nearby towns preferring to squat there out of convenience. Understandably so. The bus company, then the first of its kind in the country, was also the largest employer of Y-riga, second only to the public school system. The business enterprise was founded in the early 1900's by a Jewish immigrant driven out of Russia during the pogrom and an American soldier who had chosen to live in Bikol after the Philippine-American War. It's been run since by "imported" executives.

Still, the desolation of Bocawe was felt even by the two young explorers who were not strangers in the vicinity. It was in stark contrast to the bustling national highway where wood-framed and concrete houses as well as shops and sari-sari stores abound on both sides. But none of those dwellings were comparable to the luxury staff-houses built inside BITRANCO for its top executives. The company compound complete with such amenities as an Olympic-size swimming pool, two tennis courts and a motorbike trail, was also wholly hedged from the public by a thicket of Chinese bamboos. Yet, to all of these and many other private goings-on inside the exclusive community of non-locals the boys of kadlagan were privy. The reason for it was that along the south end of the secured and manicured enclave lay the little realm of wilderness, the kadlagan, over which Salvio and Minandro were the lords.

"LB, you like Tricia, don't you."

"Tricia Blancaflor, the daughter of the BITRANCO boss? No way, she's sexy on her bikinis but acts like a boy."

"Just because she rides a motorcycle?"

"Did you see her flipped over from the diving board? I can't even do that at brookside. She's something. Maybe you like her, HB."

"Gee, she's twice as tall as me. Besides, she only speaks English. I'm not sure I can handle that."

"Did you catch the name of the girl in purple bathing suit? Sounds like she's from Manila. She speaks *Tagalog*.

"Sonya, maybe. She has no bust."

"You know that boy—I guess he's from Manila too, he brags to the girls about his swimming. I don't think at brookside he can catch up with me."

"And I don't think he can shoot a bird with a slingshot either."

Minandro got a bit moody and then hummed The Magic Touch but inaudibly enough only he could hear.

As the morning sunlight started to brighten up the increasingly narrowing and rising dirt road, a family of Agtas emerged from a distance in front of them, marching in single file, in the background was the cogon-covered landscape that made up the expanse of the rolling foothills of Sumagang.

CHAPTER 14

In the summer, the cogon grasses are like a military phalanx formation set up strategically along the edges of the valley as Sumagang's first line of defense at the threshold of the elevation. As the army of lush verdant spears shift in unison from one formation to another at the command of the wind, the scenery becomes breathtaking. But the beauty and harmony of the drill can only be appreciated from afar. The poetry ends as soon as the lines are broken and intruders come hand to hand, body to stalk with the man-sized razor blades all ready to draw blood at contact.

The princes of kadlagan fortunately were not greenhorns. It wasn't their first time in the theater of operation either. Salvio in particular remembered how to negotiate the secret path leading to the friendlier playing fields strewn with forest flowers, dwarf coconuts and wild Java guavas. The boys followed the secret path. The morning sun was beginning to assert itself when they reached the flat upland, the jump-off point to iliyan.

At the end of the "guava plantation," as Minandro would call it, the pitch of the hill changes abruptly. It was past six o'clock in the morning, the sun was starting to scorch the hikers, and the cogon grasses were bobbing up again when the charge actually began.

An hour past since they set off from San Nicolas chapel and the weight of their backpacks was taking its toll. Minandro thought it was taking them longer this time to gain height as compared to last summer's abortive assault, although just as during the first attempt, they followed a beaten course, which was not altogether unhindered. Whenever the cogon obstructed their way, they used their arrows to par the leaves to avoid being lacerated or poked in the eye as the grass frolicked wildly with the wind. After another half hour, the first to grumble of lactic acid buildup in his calves was Minandro.

"Do you want to take a rest?" Salvio asked while offering his canteen before taking a gulp from it himself.

"You first."

"Alright."

And then Minandro took the canteen from Salvio, swallowed a mouthful and said, "Maybe we should take a break when we reach that coconut." He gestured with the same hand holding the canteen to point to a marker ahead of them, about half an hour away.

"Alright." Salvio got the container back and took another gulp.

The sun was punishing the two boys and there was no shade in sight. The ascent seemed unending and that early in the journey their morale was dwindling fast. Yet, none was complaining and the assault went on. Salvio became careless and was cut in the leg by a three-inch wide blade. The wound bled as it itched even after he'd covered it with two strips of Band-Aid.

Minandro was thirsting again but he would not ask for more water. He knew their only canteen was less than half-full and there would be no source of water on the hill. The heat was humid and oppressive, the will was there but the body was waning, and the worst had yet to come.

Then the wind let out a reluctant wheeze, followed by a shrill, and then by soft whistles coming from all directions as if in harmony with the heartbeats, the panting and the advancing trudge of the marchers. The cool breeze comforted their burning faces, the mayas performed arias in succession to becalm them further, and even the cogon grass obliged to hitch on by dancing more predictably. The pantomime lasted until the climbers finally reached their appointed marker. There, the interlude brought forth a symphonic bliss where even the exhilarating panorama below was in sync. The landscape in the valley deftly rendered itself live behind the determined duo and then effervesced in its natural splendor to the rhythm the mountaineers needed frenziedly to regain their spirits.

The respite allowed tiring muscles to recuperate although the 7:00 AM shadow of the coconut palms did not give any shelter from the sweltering sun. Resting on their backpacks and against the coconut trunk, legs spread and extended on the grass, Salvio and Minandro quietly appreciated the breathtaking beauty of nature that unfolded before them. Then, as if freshly energized they became playful again by putting the township together like pieces of puzzle on a board. One by one, they located from the scenery in the valley the exact sites of landmarks they recognized. They figured them out sans debate: the Ibana College campus, the City Hall, the Y-riga Hotel, and the Cagayunan Bldg., the tallest in town. They also came into easy consensus that the most visible serpentine line winding across the valley floor is the national highway.

"Where's kadlagan?" Minandro asked.

The question seemed unwelcome. Somewhat thrown, Minandro rose to his feet, his bow and arrows in tow, and went about the coconut after excusing himself to tap his bladder. The shrubs were momentarily pushed aside by a strong gust, and there emerged the stately Sumagang towering over iliyan on which Minandro stood. Another whiff exposed the open bosom of the mountain then partly hidden by pockets of gray clouds, but that simply added to the inscrutability of the densely wooded depths of its famous declivity, the wound that never heals. Still the commanding mass looked as far-flung from iliyan as it was from the boys' room, and yet not seemingly as insuperable. It's right there, set apart only by the cogon-carpeted trough down the valley where they set out for the climb from the opposite side earlier that morning. Minandro lost his urge to urinate. As immediately as he turned around, his eyeballs stuck out like brookside pebbles past Salvio. A snake of vile disposition was ready to strike his HB.

"Don't move, don't even breathe."

"What?"

"I said don't move. There's a cobra behind you."

Salvio was petrified. He knows how venomous mountain cobras are. He'd seen how one Agta who worked for his Itay in Hacienda Bartolome died on being envenomed by the snake. The worker was done in less than 30 minutes after profusely frothing at the mouth and convulsing, and then going into complete paralysis before expiring.

Minandro was frantically debating with himself whether to reach for his slingshot and the perfect pebble in his backpack, or use the bow and arrows he was already holding even as the benumbed Salvio was begging with his eyes for his buddy to do something pronto, now! Then Minandro dropped two arrows from his hand without a sound retaining only the one Salvio crafted for him, raised the bow firmly and cautiously, and set his weapon at the steady and frozen serpent, its deep dark evil eyes as watchful of Salvio as of him. Minandro knew the mean *rimoranon*[10] could also attack by

---

[10] *rimoranon*: Philippine cobra

spitting its venom as far as where he was standing. The cobra struck before Minandro could make a perfect aim, but the arrow still caught the intended target cutting it into halves. Salvio hurriedly rose to his feet, picked up his own bow and swung it repeatedly until it was broken on the separated creature still squiggling aimlessly on the grass.

"Stop now, HB. Stop! Now, show me your right hand."

"I got a bite," Salvio confirmed his guy's worst fear.

Salvio was resigned something would happen to him at any moment. Minandro was panicky and kicked in anger the dead meat away from them. Salvio regained his composure.

"LB, there's a bottle of alcohol in my knapsack, get it and wash the wound with it. Please hurry."

"Okay." Minandro took the alcohol out and poured it on the open tissue just below Salvio's right wrist. "I have my dad's hunting knife, HB. I will cut your skin and suck the venom out."

"Hurry, guy LB."

Minandro cut a cross on the wounded flesh and after gargling with the rubbing alcohol, sucked the blood out of the wound. Salvio passed out when Minandro spat out blood on the smudge of rimoranon meat on the ground.

"Help, help, someone help us please." Minandro's cry for succor reverberated from the mountain wall. But there was only quiet. The mayas stopped singing, the wind took a break somehow, and even the cogon grasses just stood still.

"HB, Salvio, wake up, wake up." Minandro shook his buddy on the shoulder several times. There was no response from guy HB whose face was turning white and lifeless. He gently stroked Salvio's forehead and felt that it was warm. *No, HB is not gone yet.* Minandro was definitely not ready to give up on his dear friend. He picked up the canteen hanging on the army belt Salvio was wearing and emptied its contents on his buddy's face. The sensation of drowning made Salvio sit up and cough out the water. Minandro almost fainted himself at that point.

"Water please. Please give me some water."

Minandro, still holding the canteen, shook it a bit to feel if there was still water left inside. There was none. Salvio saw what Minandro did and just closed his eyes.

"The juice, the juice will help. I have balimbing in my bag." Minandro took out the yellowest of the starfruits and offered it to Salvio. A bite, a sip, but Salvio thirsted even more.

"What about chico?"

"It's ok, LB."

"No, I'll get you some water. Just don't move there or else the venom will travel to your heart."

"I'm fine, I just need a little more rest and I'll be alright and maybe we can go on," Salvio put up a brave front to reassure his buddy.

"No, let's stay here for another hour and let's see what's gonna happen."

The sky was clear and the sun continued to scorch them with increasing ferocity, sapping them more of their energy. But Minandro thought he still had enough strength to scale the one *lanyog*[11] that has turned to be the point of extended break in their journey. He realized the file of dwarf coconuts that had lined their course was about twenty minutes below the hill, so that would be out of the question. They needed to rehydrate themselves now and the only logical way to do it was for him to climb the 60-foot lanyog and fetch coconut water, the clear juice inside young coconuts, especially for ailing HB.

"I think I know what you're thinking, LB," Salvio, still in his sick voice, guessed what Minandro had in mind. "If you're going to do it, here—have my belt and take the bayonet with you, it's in the knapsack, you know. To cut the coconut from the stalks, you need something heavier and longer than your dad's hunting knife."

Minandro wore the belt, hooked the bayonet to it and began the climb. He was up on the crown of the coconut in less than two minutes with a brief rest in between. The scrapes on the flesh of his chest and on both arms for clinging like a reptile on the branchless trunk were bleeding. It was only his second conquest of a coconut tree; the last one was in kadlagan—of a 15-foot variety.

"Good job, LB, good job."

"Thanks." And Minandro cut the first coconut from the stalk. "What the—Oh my, Oh my God. Jesus. Oh my God."

"What is it, LB, what is it?"

---

[11] *lanyog*: Coconut trees that grow up to 90 feet

"Bees, giant bees, I'm being attacked by a swarm of giant bees up here. It's all over me."

"What? Bees? LB, close your eyes, cover your nose, cover your ears." Salvio could barely see his buddy who was hidden by two layers of coconut leaves 60 feet above him.

"I can't, I can't. I can't stand it. They're all over me, stinging me everywhere. My head, my face, my arms, everywhere!"

"LB jump out or they'll kill you."

"I can't, my hands, my legs are numbed."

"Just jump LB, over there, on the cogon grass. What if you break a leg, they'll kill you anyway up there. So jump, jump now!"

Minandro gathered his composure and somehow managed to kick the beehive where it was nestled and as it crashed down the ground the swarm flew off into the open field.

Then there was silence.

"LB, what's going on up there? Please tell me. I can't see you from here."

"I guess the bees are gone, HB," Minandro was a bit sarcastic.

"And you?"

"I guess I'm swollen in every inch of me, I can't open my right eye. I'm—a bit dizzy, otherwise I'm okay."

"So come down now."

"Not yet, I have to finish this thing." Minandro struggled in pain using the bayonet, that had been useless to stave off the onslaught of the bees, to sever off the young coconuts from their yolk stalks. And then the coconuts came down one after another.

After a while, Minandro dismounted from the crown of the tree and finally climbed down. Salvio thought he saw a gorilla coming out of the mist.

"Is that you, LB?"

"Oh yeah."

"Minandro, are you okay?" Salvio wanted a truthful answer.

"Swell. I'm swell."

CHAPTER 15

For one long moment, the dog-tired boys stared blank either at the green coconuts that rolled to the bushes or at the long winding trail down the hill. And lying slumped against the base of the lanyog, they seemed like infantrymen drained of their last strength after a successful defense of their trench. Then Salvio rose slowly to his feet, limped towards the bushes and picked up two coconuts. Minandro was still motionless except for the movements of his eyes following Salvio. With the bayonet, Salvio cut off a piece of the coconut husk in a perfect stroke by the hand wounded by the snake bite and then exposed a hole on it with a second blow on the same spot. Although really feeling done in, he did the same thing to the other coconut and offered it to his buddy. Minandro did not hesitate, got hold of the coconut now ready to drink, and forthwith sucked the juice with his gorilla lips still inflamed from the stings of the bees. Salvio also finished up his, and afterwards whacked the coconuts into halves; they used the maiden cut of the husk to scoop up the tender white flesh inside the woody shell and slurp it.

Somewhat refreshed, Minandro was talking again and became engrossed again with the landscape before them: "If that's the church, the one on the left should be the Armand Theater."

"Here, LB, use the binoculars."

"Oh yes, thanks. Let me see now—" Minandro took the telescopes from Salvio without hesitation and, with it, scanned the scenery below.

"So, is it better? What do we have this time?"

"Oh well, we're wrong all the while. We're actually looking at Bua earlier because there's the Bua Lake, I'm sure. And Y-riga is out there, to the far left of the lake. I could see the Ibana College and the church, the belfry—"

"May I see?" Salvio was curious and excited himself.

"Wait HB, I'm looking for kadlagan. What the—I'm lost here. I just can't figure it out. Oh well, ok, here you can have your binoculars." Salvio grabbed the binoculars back from Minandro who couldn't hide his frustration.

"Yes, I can see the Ibana campus myself LB," Salvio assured his friend somewhat. "And wow the church too! Now, where's BITRANCO? If we can find BITRANCO, we can find kadlagan. But, hey, everything is just green out there, just trees and forest. Where the heck is it?"

Then, there was quiet. How could such a terrain especially favored by nature, invested with so much emotion, the seat of grand exploits and the keeper of boyhood memoirs be lost in the mix?

That's just stupid!

The sun was being ruthless again in the midst of the puzzlement and in the long silence of the wind. Minandro turned his attention uphill and reckoned it would take them another half an hour to reach the peak of iliyan. He was still sore from the lanyog misadventure and noticed his limbs were still reddened. Affectionately vetting his Salvio, he found him normal, but not in his jaunty disposition yet. Salvio, on the other hand, caught the deportment of his friend and thought of something to divert him.

"LB, do you see those coconuts beyond the bushes?" Salvio pointed a finger westward down the hill. "That's our plantation. I've been there a couple of times with cousin Efren. We always had fun playing with the Agtas although they're shy most of the time. It's just like kadlagan."

"You own the plantation?"

"Itay said the land and everything that grows there belong to his people."

"What people? Is your Itay like Mayor Magbanua who is the leader of the Y-riga people?"

"I guess something like that. Itay said our ancestors have lived there since the beginning, and they had been a happy people because Sumagang protected them."

"Wait a minute, if the people who have lived there own it since the beginning, how come I hear your family call the iliyan property as Hacienda Bartolome?

"I really don't know, but I think Judge Torda helped Itay prepare some papers to get that name."

"Hey HB, your skin is dark just like your Itay, Don Patricio, and your hair is wavy, does that mean that you have Agta blood?"

"Does it matter to you, LB?"

"Does it matter to me? Why should it matter to me? Anyway, is that why you make the perfect Y for our slingshots and the perfect bows and arrows?"

"Our Agta friends showed us, Efren and me, how."

"Why doesn't your Itay make himself the mayor of your hacienda, of iliyan and of Sumagang so he can be as powerful as Mayor Magbanua and his bother Warlito?"

"Itay said what is important is education and education is power."

"Didn't you tell me before that Agtas pray to Sumagang? Do they still do that?"

"I guess. Even Itay prays to Sumagang often."

"Now I know why Don Patricio doesn't go to church. Can I tell my parents that you are Agta?"

"No, please, Itay won't want it. Keep it a secret. Our secret. Anyways, I hope Ma'am Monteverde will let you go with me, Efren and Itay to the plantation before the summer ends."

"If my mother found out about the blanket, I'd be done for the summer, HB."

"So, let's not plant the flag anymore. Let's just head home now. We are getting very tired and weak anyway."

Minandro took a long poignant look first at the peak of iliyan and then beyond it, at the imposing heights of Sumagang, and said: "If we go home now without finishing what we set out to do I'd be nothing. We are nothing."

"Well, ok, if you are going, I'm going. But first, let's have more coconut juice."

The last stage of the climb took the climbers longer to ascend than they had anticipated as the sharp angle of inclination towards the top of iliyan made their advance uphill even more grueling. They were also driving their last assault in the sweltering heat of the mid-noon sun. When they finally summited, the spent mountaineers were forthwith refueled and recharged as though by a flash of fresh and interconnected chemistry. They forgot about their pains, their exhaustion; instead, they moved in concert wasting not a second to set up their edifice of conquest. First, Salvio whipped out the blanket they brought with them from his knapsack and together quickly unfolded it on the grass. Salvio found the cloth oversized, so he cut it into two pieces. He bundled up with a string his three arrows together to serve as the flagpole, and then they worked to fasten to it two ends of the cut fabric. Minandro chopped Salvio's broken bow into four pieces to use them as supports for the base of the stand. They literally raced to plant the staff into the ground with great gusto and even as they were firmly fortifying it, the flag proudly unfurled itself into the air; it could not wait to flap and flutter to the adulation of the wind. The job finished, Minandro momentarily looked askance at the distant Sumagang, then took a few measured steps back from the flagpole, perked his head up and saluted at the flag as Salvio watched him in awe in that look again. Then Salvio snapped his own salute.

CHAPTER 16

Minandro, neat, tall and handsome in his polo-barong, black trousers and Glenmore leather shoes, snapped his right hand down after saluting Manila Mayor Arsenio to pick up the handshake offered by the mayor. Salvio in the same attire, his grin wide and innocent, remained in full salute. He missed out his morning business class at Colegio de San Juan because Antonio could not make it to the ceremony. Then the mayor extended his hand in the same fashion to Salvio being the next in line. "No, I'm standing in for his parents," Salvio demurred. The buddies, both a bit embarrassed yet all gleaming, winked at each other like old time and promptly proceeded to their respective seats, Minandro to join the members of Batch 21, the newest additions to the Manila's Finest and Salvio to the area reserved for the families of the inductees. The event was the official commissioning of 300 or so fresh graduates of the Manila Police Academy. The venue was the famous Maharlika Gallery of the City Hall. It was summer of 1968.

The two skipped the photo-ops with the mayor, hurried down the street and took a jeepney ride back to Minandro's boarding house in Sampaloc, Manila.

"We need to wait for Antonio there until he dismisses his class at noontime," Minandro explained.

"His class at Santo Domingo University?"

"Yes, and we will be joined in by the gang."

Antonio actually organized the party at the urgings of proud town mates to celebrate the occasion of the second ever native Y-rigueño becoming a police officer of the nation's capital.

The group flagged two taxi cabs. "San Mig, please," Antonio directed the driver after Salvio and Minadro hopped in. No sooner had their taxi negotiated the side streets of Manila for the shortest route to the beerhouse than Salvio saw Frankie from the other car following them frantically waving a newspaper. At the traffic light an unkempt newsboy, one of Manila's working urchins, held up the afternoon tabloid in front of them. The banner: **Mayor Arsenio inducts 300 more riot police**. The picture on the front page: Minandro in firm handshake with the mayor of Manila, Salvio in the background executing a grand salute. Salvio showed his wide grin again and acknowledged Frankie with a thumbs-up which engendered a discord of cheer inside the other taxi. Antonio quietly congratulated his brother.

At the San Mig Garden, at first they spoke in Y-riga in lowered tones and ordered their beer and *pulutan*[12] in Tagalog. The group soon became rowdy as the night passed. One town mate called for the manager of the beerhouse to come over and hinted at him, flaunting the picture on the newspaper, if the next round could be on the house "to honor the promotion of Sergeant Monteverde." The honoree although somewhat irked ignored the brashness of his town mate but Salvio cut him politely and apologized to the manager.

"That's Letty now," Frankie announced, pointing to the topless dancer on the narrow platform in the middle of the beer garden. "The sweet little girl, the daughter of hmm—Demetrio, you know, Demetrio the BITRANCO driver, the deadbeat who lived on Bocawe on the far end of the road to iliyan, remember?"

"That's her? Oh my—," was the subdued chorus.

The mention of iliyan suddenly dampened the celebratory mood of Salvio and Minandro. While the rest of the gang ogled at the scantily clad girls parading on the ramp, the two began to be as much engrossed in a hushed private chat as Antonio, although his eyes transfixed at the exotic dancers, was also absorbed in a different world.

---

[12] *pulutan*: Finger food

"I'm sure what I saw was a wild boar in the brush," Minandro's voice rose a bit. "We were then very exhausted alright, but not in such a state to fantasize things," Minandro went on recollecting to his friend the tragic scene on their descent from iliyan 11 years ago that wouldn't go away.

"I didn't see the damn pig myself but I remember you following the movement in the grove with your arrow and then you took a shot. We were very nervous and waited for a while before checking out."

Both remembered they had cautiously approached the thicket with their knives drawn, and found out that right behind the trees and wild grass was a deep pit. They looked down expecting to find a dead boar but they were shocked to discover instead a man sprawled in a prone position at the bottom of the pit, motionless, lifeless, the head covered with blood and beside the body was the arrow Minandro shot into the brush. Since then, Minandro has not been the same again.

"What the heck he was hiding in the grass from?" Minandro posed that same question again.

"Maybe answering a call of nature?"

"Up in iliyan?"

That ended the conversation as Minandro felt the urge to answer his own call and headed for the men's room. He had other things spinning in his mind besides.

As the night passed, the gang became louder except Antonio. The roving disco lights betrayed, time and again, his sullen eyes even in the dim premises of the beer garden. He was taciturn all evening and Salvio noticed him still sipping his first bottle of beer.

"What's the problem guy?" Salvio asked Antonio from across the table. "Your pa?"

"Yes," Antonio didn't hesitate. Then he went on to indulge in his own thoughts.

The day after Edgardo had been abducted, his anxious mother came to see Leo. She confronted the professor on the hallway with a certain air of familiarity as soon as he got out of his class. They had known each other at University of the Philippines having worked together as staff members of the literary guild. They were in fact school sweethearts at the outbreak of the war.

"Leo, my son Edgardo did not come home last night and I haven't heard from him. I learned that Warlito's men carried him out of your class. Is that true?"

"Glad to see you Elena," he greeted and kissed her on the cheek. "I'm sorry but I'm very worried myself."

She pushed him back and demanded an answer, "Did you do anything, and have you done anything about it?"

"Yes, Elena. I talked to Chief Enriquez before coming to class this morning. He said no one brought Edgardo to the police station. And then he gave me his own worried look but with the assurance he'll have the matter looked into and let me know if anything that I should know comes up."

"Did you believe him?"

"No. But I tried to place a call to General Ablan in Manila to get some help. He's a friend of mine. His wife said he's out of the country, unfortunately."

"What are we gonna do? Will you come with me now to see the mayor?"

"It may be futile my dear Elena. When it comes to Warlito's madness — I dunno, I just dunno. Well, those men are also the Mayor's, I know, but they are *estrangeros*. They are not from Y-riga, no one knows their identities, their names. And who will dare testify against them? Who will defy Warlito in this town?"

"You, Leo. You. You are the only one Warlito respects in this town. He used to idolize you. He dreads your guts."

The professor looked at the woman in front of him directly in the eye—that same Monteverde look which spooks Salvio whenever Minandro wears it—and said, "I promise I'll do something about it. Go home now, Elena."

She drew him to her and they embraced tightly.

Antonio was at hand when the confrontation between his father and Warlito took place inside the Ibana campus. He was in fact querying his father about the case of Edgardo as they were leisurely treading the covered walkway towards the Liberal Arts building when they saw Warlito and his men coming their way. Warlito was in the campus with two bodyguards to fetch his girlfriend who was teaching at the high school. Leo grabbed the opportunity.

"Lito, can we talk for a second?

"Yeah, prof what's up?"

"It's about my student, Edgardo, Lito."

"Stop there, right now Leo because I have no time for it. We are in a hurry. My girlfriend and I have an important event to attend."

Leo dogged Warlito. "Your men carried him off during my class yesterday, I mean forcibly snatched him from his seat, inside my classroom, while I was teaching, and he has not been heard from since then. Do you still have Edgardo?"

"Whose men are you talking about? And lay off me right now, I told you I'm busy. And don't be a fool."

"Let's be reasonable. Please tell me, what did Edgardo do to deserve it?"

At that very juncture, Warlito attempted to draw his Colt .45 from his waist but, before he could make any threat with his firearm, Leo took it away from him in a flash. Disarmed Warlito turned ashen. Then Leo ordered Warlito's stunned bodyguards to drop their guns to the ground and take a hike. The henchmen were confused.

"Leave now or I'll blow his brains off," Leo's voice was firmer this time as he pressed the pistol harder to Warlito's head. "Last warning, gentlemen."

"Go, go," Warlito directed his men. "Just wait for me at the gate." The two men started to leave by walking backwards first, hands still holding their undrawn handguns.

"I said go, move, faster," Warlito ordered his men again. "We'll finish this quickly."

Meanwhile, Antonio was literally ossified while the drama was taking place. There were a couple more of Ibana students who were equally taken aback on recognizing the parties involved in the commotion. "Isn't that Sir Monteverde?" one asked. That was the first time Antonio saw his father's tricks although he knew a lot of his guerilla exploits during the last war from the pundits of Coty's Store and from Professor Palma himself. He also learned from the sari-sari store pundit, Mr. de la Rama, that at the height of the resistance movement his father and now General Ablan had been given a mission by the Kanlaon Guerrilla Unit to take out a high-placed Japanese collaborator in Manila, a senator, but the mission was aborted because of the sudden death of the target owing to natural cause.

When Warlito's bodyguards were gone, Leo clicked the magazine out first before returning the gun to Warlito.

"You're dead Leo, you know that. All for that little commie? What a waste."

"But tell me first where the little commie is right now," Leo gave Warlito a collar choke and imposed his resoluteness on the subdued and humiliated rogue but who remained defiant, at least verbally.

"I don't know mister professor. Maybe up there in Sumagang. That's where he always wanted to be. Find him there."

"Did you take him there?" Leo tightened his grip.

"But why should that be your problem," Warlito taunted his tormentor. "Your problem now is you. Consider yourself dead meat unless you pack up very soon and join your friends and dinosaurs like you in the mountain. Fool."

The day after, a student of Ibana College came to the Monteverde residence at dusk and brought the tragic news to the family that Professor Leo Monteverde was taken to the hospital with several gunshot wounds.

CHAPTER 17

The rowdiness of the gang in San Mig Garden, well into the wee hours of the morning, has not bedimmed the events of more than a decade ago that Salvio reviewed in his mind.

The day was well-nigh done when he and Minandro reached the guava plantation. On the horizon, the nocturnal bats in rapid, jagged aerial twists and turns began to forage for prey in flight. The flying little mammals, maybe hundreds of them are tenants in the attic of the Monteverde residence, took over the still crimson sky from the elegant swallows that swooped down for the final meal of the day. As darkness fell, Salvio became more cautious and watchful in every step on the lightly trodden path towards home, making sure that those twigs and cogon stems on the ground were not rimoranon lying in ambush. Minandro was tongue-tied for the most part during their hurried and tense descent from iliyan, his mind dominated by the gruesome image of the dead man in the pit. It didn't take long at all for Salvio to figure out his friend's unusual countenance.

"Gee, LB, you are not going to jail," Salvio broke the ice as they walked at a more normal pace on the plains. "No one saw what happened, we know it was an accident and you are not even 14 years old. Okay?"

Minandro ignored the consolation.

"Guy, listen now," Salvio persisted, "you should worry more about how you could get away with missing dinner time again, and maybe getting flapped by Ma'am."

That shook up Minandro who lost no time to whip out his dad's hunting knife, wiped it on his shirt and examined his image on one side of the blade. *Oh my, ma will think I've been into a fight again.*

"Not bad, believe me LB," Salvio assured his pal.

"Okay, I'll just explain I'd been stung by bees and decided to stay in your house until I looked better," Minandro finally uttered something in complete sentence.

"There you go, LB, Ma'am Monteverde will take that excuse. Problem's solved."

"No, it's not—maybe, that, yes."

But, but a man, a dead man in the pit is not some unlucky game in the wild or a poor malapaga blasted dead by a sling shot. Minadro's thoughts continued to give him the willies. He could be some else's friend, son or father.

There was momentary silence.

Or cousin. Salvio at that juncture remembered Efren who's been missing for five days already. Efren usually let

Salvio know his whereabouts whenever he had stowed away before. But why not this time?

At 7:00 PM on a Holy Wednesday at the last leg of their trek back home, the two boys found Bocawe to be eerily dark and desolate. The quirky placidness was broken only by the intermittent barking of dogs and the lamentation of Pasyon emanating from two or more huts on both sides of the dirt road. The chants of professional *pasyonistas* were plaintive and mournful yet reticent and reverential. Minandro had once related to Salvio how he could hear them from the boys' room every *Semana Santa* and also when there's death in the neighborhood. But this was the first time ever he felt so close to the reality of death. *Doesn't he deserve a funeral hymn too?* On the other hand, Salvio could sense the scene of the dead man in the pit was racing in Minandro's mind again. As they hit the national highway, Salvio could only hope the haunting would cease when his buddy would start concocting some explanation to Mrs. Monteverde at home, just a couple of houses away.

"Guy Salvio, why is our house so dark?" Minandro was alarmed by what he saw as the two of them passed through the arching kalachuchi at the entrance of the Monteverde residence. "Where is everybody?" At that point, Minandro felt a spasm of disquietude in the pit of his stomach. Something's really wrong.

"I dunno, Minandro. Your dining room is always lighted at this time. Yes, something's not really right here."

Minandro rushed towards the narra door with Salvio in tow to find out what's going inside the house. He was about to strike the door when it suddenly swung open. One of the maids turned up, crying.

"What's going on? Where are they? Why did you turn off all the lights?"

"Ma'am Ymelda told us to turn off the lights."

"Why? What's wrong? Where's Ma, where's Pa, Antonio, Rebecca?"

"In the hospital."

"Why?"

"Sir Leo was shot."

"Pa was shot? Oh my God. Shot by who and which hospital?"

Not sure, sir."

"Which hospital? *Tonta!*[13]"

"Maybe Lourdes, yes Lourdes—I think, sir."

"Tonta. Why can't you be sure? Stupid!"

Minandro without waiting for an answer ran back to the highway followed by Salvio. He tried to flag down a tricycle at least three times, and each time he was ignored added to the trepidation inside him that was about to implode. Salvio was near tears watching his buddy cursing and panicking but kept his cool.

"LB, let's just run, Lourdes Hospital is not that far, we'll be there in half an hour."

---

[13] *tonta*: Bonehead

"Alright, okay, let's go," Minandro concurred in the suggestion without thinking.

And the two dashed towards the poblacion, with Minandro still in full battle gear: the oversized bow slung across his chest, two deadly arrows tucked in his knapsack, hunting knife dangling from his belt and slingshot, with the handsome snake handle, hanging around his neck.

No sooner Salvio was asking the lady in the front desk Mr. Leo Monteverde's room number.

"But you can't be in this hospital like that," the lady addressed Minandro, who was standing behind his friend.

"Mr. Monteverde is my father. I'm his son. I want to see him right now."

"Well, sir, you have to leave your stuff here before you could go inside. Besides, the patient is still in the ER."

Minandro was still arguing with the front desk lady when his mother and his sister, Rebecca, arms wrapped around her mother's waist and sobbing, came out of the hallway.

"Ma, what happened to Papa, where's he, is he ok?" Minandro anxiously directed his questions to his mother.

Mrs. Monteverde took a pause for a moment and carefully inspected the sunburned and unkempt Minandro from head to foot in such wonderment her son's question did not seem to register with her at all.

Gee, now she knows they have been in iliyan. That's how Salvio read Mrs. Monteverde's reaction.

But Mrs. Monteverde had another thing going for her and she didn't know whether to rebuke or pity her 12-year old son, all geared up to be a party to a perilous adult matter.

"No, Minandro, no more violence, enough. Let the law take its course."

Salvio a bit confused, checked the appearance of his buddy again and then felt relieved on realizing what Mrs. Monteverde actually meant.

"LB, please give me your things, go see your pa."

"Thanks, Salvio." Minandro lost no time at all slipping himself off his contraptions.

"I know where pa is," Rebecca, still sobbing, volunteered and led his brother to the ER.

Salvio first gathered his buddy's stuff in a corner and followed the two while Mrs. Monteverde went outside the entrance lobby of the hospital and turned her quizzical eyes toward Mt. Sumagang.

When the three of them entered the ER, Antonio was staring at the ceiling, maybe praying, while Mr. Monteverde lay pale and unconscious on the bed, breathing only through an opening cut through his neck. Minandro quietly repaired to his pa and touched his hand. Antonio noticing the presence of his brother came closer to the bed and put his hands on his brother's shoulders. No words were exchanged, Minandro just touching his father's hand without holding it and Antonio gently brushing his brother's shoulders.

"Mom said Warlito did it," Rebecca made a casual announcement. "And if Pa makes it, the doctor told mom, he'll be paralyzed from the waist down."

CHAPTER 18

Ymelda left her children grieving over the hapless condition of their father without letting them know. Outside the hospital that adjoins the national highway, she hailed a tricycle coming from Sumagang's direction towards the poblacion. She was ignored.

The town center is a 30-minute stride from Lourdes Hospital. But at nighttime, it is not a walk in the park to many Y-rigueños. There's a building on that stretch of the highway, the old Buenviaje house, between the hospital and Armand Theatre, that they believe is haunted. During World War II, the Japanese converted the building into a military post where Y-rigueños suspected of being guerillas were tortured to death. In front of the house is an old acacia whose branches dangerously hang across the highway. A *kapre,* a hairy and tobacco-smoking ten-foot tree demon playing pranks on passersby, women especially, older folks swear inhabit the tree and, it is also believed, guard the souls of the tortured still trapped in the building. But what's actually of concern to Ymelda as she surveyed the roadway ahead of her were the kikig, the water snakes that regularly paddle out of their aquatic existence from brookside, on the opposite side of the house, perhaps in a nightly suicidal slog across the road to prove their terrestrial roots. The reptiles, carrion or alive, litter that most dreaded part of the highway.

Ymelda decided to just go on foot and brave the unlit highway when another tricycle rattled off past her and sped up into the night. Her eyes followed the motorized velocipede nonchalantly, her stolid face hiding the trepidations inside.

No dumb witness would come out against Warlito. The police would just file a slipshod report, and it's hopeless to rely on Judge Torda, the chicken-hearted.

Susmaryosep! *I will settle this myself, with Rufino.*

Mayor Rufino Magbanua, Pino to Ymelda since high school, was one of Ymelda's very first suitors, along with Judge Torda and Patricio Bartolome. He belongs to an old political family and the town's landed gentry but whose folkways are considered barriotic. Rufino and Ymelda were childhood playmates since the Magbanua residence is just three blocks from the ancestral home of Ymelda in San Joaquin. In many ways, Rufino was the antipode of his rogue brother, Warlito. Dandy and mannerly, he was also idolized in San Joaquin, by the young women in the barrio in particular, as their Beau Brummel.

San Joaquin, the next barrio east of poblacion, begins at the first major intersection of the City. The townspeople call the intersection *canto*, specifically the corner of the dirt path to San Joaquin and the highway that leads directly to the Church on the far left side, to the City Hall and then the poblacion.

The most prominent structure of the canto is the Cagayunan Bldg. in which the "bad guys" of San Joaquin have been permanent fixtures. The locals call them *canto* boys, the toughest and baddest of them served as a ready pool for Warlito's recruits.

The canto boys were the secret lovers of Ymelda who blossomed into full womanhood early; they assigned themselves as her protectors. But no sooner youngsters from poblacion, the *centro* boys from the merchant and professional breed, began to notice her eclectic charms. Yet before they could render their *harana*, the nocturnal courtship songs, to Ymelda in San Joaquin, these young suitors must be gutsy enough to go beyond the canto, the passage to San Joaquin. The alternative route is a 25-mile trek on the rebel-infested section of Sumagang that winds up in Bantog, the town at the other end of San Joaquin.

To the folks of San Joaquin, Ymelda's mother, Nana Guring, a sought-after prayer leader in the whole barrio for novenas, litanies and prayers for the dead, is a pious catholic

111

extraordinaire. The canto boys therefore have respected Nana Guring as much as they have been jealous of Ymelda. Little is known however that her mother, Juliana, had reverted to animism before giving birth to Guring. Juliana was a victim of repeated sexual assaults; her tormentor was Padre Son Tua, the "Chinese" curate of the neighboring pueblo of Bua. Padre Son Tua never admitted his paternity of Guring but he provided for her and raised her to strict Hispanic Catholicism when Juliana lost her sanity.

The ever devout Guring always in her best *kimona, saya* and *bakya*[14] would go to the four o'clock mass virtually every single morning—except only when prevented by illness. She went by herself most of the time, or with Ymelda. Their house in San Joaquin is about three miles distant from the church. When Ymelda missed the early morning mass, she would attend the five o'clock mass in the afternoon and by then the canto boys would be up and around, from their hangover the night before, to be delighted every time the virginal "Damsel of San Joaquin" strolled alone in regal gait by the Cagayunan Bldg. on her way to church.

The teen-aged Ymelda was no dainty lassie at all. She was as pious as Nana Guring, and dutiful, bookworm and disarmingly pretty without question, but she was also proud to call herself a woodworker. She learned the trade from her

---

[14] *kimona*: Embroidered blouse; *saya*: Skirt; *bakya*: Wooden slippers

father, the son of a *guardia civil* and an *India*[15] from Muslim South, known in San Joaquin as a master carpenter and a virtuoso woodcraftsman. The ornate narra door of the house in San Nicolas is a handiwork of Ymelda, *the carpenter's daughter*, which she crafted at age13.

Should Ymelda Monteverde survive the ordeal of water snakes on the national highway, her trip to barrio San Joaquin would then be a cakewalk into a friendly territory. She did, without a thud. Not for Salvio who decided to shadow her.

The figure that emerged out of the darkened highway, against the moonlit silhouette of Sumagang was unmistakable to Warlito's old-time henchmen even from afar. The fairy-like stride, her dread of the little creepers on the path notwithstanding, had been a familiar scene to the furtive admirers of Ymelda—well, until Leo spirited their damsel away to San Nicolas. Rufino had mourned the elopement of Ymelda with Leo Monteverde. For years, he had plotted to retrieve Ymelda from Leo and even considered murdering her "abductor," and Ymelda knew about it. Rufino's sinister design was however overtaken by events, the Japanese occupation of Y-riga, when Leo became a dreaded guerilla leader.

---

[15] *India*: A female native

From their strategic stations at Cagayunan Bldg., the canto boys gave out signs to each other to alert Warlito. Salvio saw what was happening and sensed danger. He stopped following his teacher right before being fully exposed by the light coming from the lamppost by the Armand Theatre, and then got off the highway, sneaked down the ditch, and waded in the chest-deep, BITRANCO oil-contaminated, snake-filled waters of brookside, both hands holding up Minandro's bow and arrows. A lost baby kikig wriggled too close for comfort; he snapped it up unexcitedly and stuck the poor reptile in his knapsack (he had two more pet-crawlers of the same kind stashed in an ink box under his bed).

Salvio thought of Minandro upon reaching the murky covered watercourse where the brook winds through. *I wish LB is with me.*

But there's no turning back. He has got to do it. Without his LB, he gathered enough guts to negotiate the dark, dingy gutter-pipe past Cagayunan Bldg.

Dripping from a mix of water, filth and oil slick, Salvio came out of the hole of the canal now running along San Joaquin. And to complete his camouflage, he rubbed the black oil from his body on his face before hiding behind a row of wild shrubs on the bank of the ditch.

Now, peeking through the bushes, Salvio saw one of Warlito's men approach Ymelda.

"Lito wants to have a word with you, Ma'am Ymelda. Please come," the man asked.

Ymelda looked at the rogue directly in the eye. He melted. Without saying a word or showing any expression, she walked past the man frozen in his post although she quickened her pace upon hitting the dirt road to San Joaquin.

Sumagang is watching him watching me and my every move from that building. Hijodeputa!

She knew too that neither the coward Warlito nor his meanest henchman could touch her.

Weakling! Coward! You recoiled and howled like a babe when Pino smacked you in the face. She found herself recalling an incident when Rufino, then a student at Ibana College courting Ymelda, had given Warlito a backhand in the nose when he caught his sibling flirting, giving her a naughty look. That was the first time Ymelda saw the darker side of the prim and proper Rufino. I will kill you, anybody who will mess around with Ymelda, Rufino bluffed and blustered and the younger brother flinched shamelessly. She remembered distinctly.

Is Rufino in it too? Ymelda hazarded a hunch. He always wanted to hurt Leo ever since their elopement.

Warlito saw everything that happened on the street. Furious because his toughest hireling had been disarmed by a mere stare, he summoned his newest recruit to do the job. Luis, a seventeen-year old OXO gang member from Naga, has been out on bail for attempted murder of a rival gang member.

"Luisito, see that woman down there walking by the lamppost," Warlito said pointing to Ymelda from Cagayunan Bldg. "She's on her way to Manoy Pino, the Mayor, my brother, you know, to make her case—that woman has a way of getting what she wants from my brother, and I will look like a moronic thug to Manoy Pino. That means trouble for us."

"Yes, I see her and I understand, Sir Lito."

"Get her up here, by any means—dead or alive."

"Yes, Sir Lito."

Luis swooped down the stairway and taking the back alley darted way past the lamppost to ambush Ymelda in the dark. In a minute, Ymelda came within the range of his attack and after briefly lying in wait on the road he made his charge like a panther and knocked down the not so unsuspecting victim.

The juvenile hooligan immediately overwhelmed Ymelda and was ready to bash her head when he felt a sharp projectile violently impelled into his neck. Blood from the cut jugular vein freely had oozed and soaked the lady's shirt before the wounded assailant fell to the ground. Ymelda, wholly dumbfounded, did not even have the change to yell for help.

"Come Ma'am Ymelda and please hurry, Warlito will soon be coming for you."

"Who are—Salvio, is that you? What happened?"

"You've been attacked Ma'am—"

"Oh my god, I have blood all over me. What happened? Who, who did this to me?"

116

"Just come Ma'am, hurry, they're coming."

Ymelda, still dazed, struggled to get up. Salvio lost no time leading her towards the ditch and into the gutter-pipe that would take them back to brookside.

"Ma'am, I'm sorry for taking you to this filthy place but we'd both get hurt if we didn't do it."

Ymelda must have lost consciousness momentarily upon hitting her head on the pavement during the assault, but now she started to recall details of what transpired.

"You shot him with that arrow—you shot him in the neck with that arrow, did you Salvio?" Ymelda wanted some answers on noticing the bow and arrows Salvio was carrying.

"I had no choice Ma'am Ymelda but shoot. The man was about to smash you to death. He had a stone in his hand."

"And why were you there in the first place?"

"I followed you from Lourdes Hospital, Ma'am. I thought Minandro would want me to follow you."

"And protect me with those weapons?"

"Yes, Mrs. Monteverde. Honestly, Ma'am."

"And what happened to that man, dead? You killed a man?"

"He is not a man, he's a boy, I mean, a teen-aged man, one of the canto boys. And I'm not exactly sure what happened to him. He first dropped beside you when he took the arrow in his throat and then rolled down the canal on the other side of the road."

"A fourth-grade pupil killed a teen-aged boy who wanted to kill his teacher, what's happening with our town, Salvio?

"No, Ma'am. He was ordered to finish off my teacher by someone who shot her husband, the father of my best friend. But, but Ma'am, no one saw anything. We are okay."

"Are you sure no one was a witness to it?

CHAPTER 19

Salvio was right about his warning to his teacher. Warlito Magbanua and his hirelings rushed to the street when Luis had not shown up to signal that his mission was accomplished. One thought petrified Warlito: Ymelda outsmarted and eluded Luis and she's now on the way to the house of his brother Rufino.

"Lito, look here. It's Luis," one of his men hollered nervously.

"Who did this? Who the devil did this to him?" Warlito was enraged at the sight of the dead Luis in the canal with eyes open and neck impaled with an arrow.

Then everyone hushed when they heard a click of a firearm coming from the thick cluster of shrubs in the woods alongside the street. Warlito drew his handgun and fired at the direction of the noise. Two of his men drew their guns too and fired at the same direction. Then a volley of gunfire was returned from the woods to the great confoundment of Warlito and his crew. The exchange of more gunshots lasted for about ten minutes. There had been gang wars between the canto boys and the centro boys on the same street before, but nothing of this sort has ever taken place and terrorized the entire neighborhood. Salvio and Ymelda were already wading the murky waters of brookside when they heard it. First Ymelda had thought the shots were intended for them until she realized they were already too far from the actual scene of the firefight. The fright and frenzy made Ymelda wholly unmindful of the little creepers in the waters that she so dreaded.

The morning of Maundy Thursday, Y-rigueños in the poblacion woke up to an eerie sense of unholiness. Outside the Municipal Building, a long queue of curious snoopers began to form. They were eager to gawk at the bodies of those slain in the firefight that were laid down side by side on the floor of the Main Entrance Hall. Among those in line was Professor Salvador Palma.

Up in the building the kibitzers were routed straight to the main hall to keep them from going the opposite direction towards Mayor Magbanua's office where the atmosphere inside was perceivably somber. There, the still unscrubbed body of Warlito Magbanua, the brother of the mayor, was placed on a conference table in the anteroom, pending autopsy by the municipal health officer. Two uniformed policemen were posted on each side of the table while some members of the Magbanua family were huddled in the private chamber of the mayor's office.

The official report that came was that rebels in the Bikol region based in Mt. Sumagang executed an early evening Holy Wednesday raid of Y-riga, the region's third largest municipality. There were seven casualties on the side of the rebels but the town lost 14 citizen army volunteers including the Mayor's brother who led the valiant defense of their town. An innocent bystander, a professor of a local college was wounded in the crossfire. The rebels used every weapon at their disposal such as Russian-made automatic assault rifles, firearms of World War II vintage and even traditional bows and arrows.

Mr. Palma left the municipal hall totally befuddled. He could not make sense at all of the decision of Kumander Diliman to conduct the raid that cost his life and his best people.

It's reckless, serves no purpose whatsoever. Dimwit, cheap cribber, goddamn bogus! Mr. Palma was ready to implode. *I thought he was different and knew better. It will take a long time before the movement recoups its loss. It's dumb, dumb!*

He proceeded immediately to Lourdes Hospital to pay a visit to Leo. Maybe Leo could help him figure out the puzzle. He really hoped nothing severe happened to him. The buzz at the municipal hall about what happened to Leo during the raid was skimpy and so conflicting.

At the hospital, only Antonio was in the critical ward where his father was transferred. Prof. Palma found his friend still in serious condition and the young man ruminative and frazzled but certainly not pitiable. The hardihood of a Monteverde has remained in him during all the trying hours, he thought. Ymelda was fond of telling her co-teachers that Antonio got the cerebral genes of his father, and Minandro the rogue oddballs. Maybe, not at this time.

"Have you been keeping watch since last night?" Mr. Palma asked cupping his hand over Antonio's, lingering on it tightly for a few seconds.

Antonio knuckled away his dried tears, looked up and nodded without saying a word.

"Tony, go home and wash up. I can take your place for now."

The nascent ideological disposition of Antonio often clashed with the political pontification of the professor, but he knew that his father would entrust the safety of the Monteverde family in his long-time comrade. Mr. Palma and Leo had been childhood chums, attended the same college and belonged to the same guerilla unit fighting the Japanese. They had done so many things together their wives have not known or will never know. Antonio therefore welcomed the offer to relieve him, but he found that very moment opportune too to first clarify certain things.

"Please tell me very honestly what's going on, Tito Sal," Antonio opened up in a muzzled tone.

"Yes, to be honest, I don't know a lot of what's going on, not yet. I don't know who did this to your father although I have strong suspicion who. Now, do you know that another terrible thing occurred last night?"

"All I know is what's going around in this hospital. They said Warlito is dead. Other details are sketchy."

"Before I go on, where are they, Ymelda, Minandro and Rebecca?" Mr. Palma expressed his concern as if he were just another member of the Monteverde family.

'They are in Don Patricio's house. Last night Ma said Warlito was out to kill her too."

"Why did you decide to stay here?"

"I had nothing to fear. I was ready for Warlito," Antonio replied feeling the outline of his father's revolver tucked in his waist.

"I don't understand why Warlito wanted to kill your mom last light."

"Me either. Ma said she'll explain. But they had to go. Salvio went with them."

"Rufino and his handlers are manipulating the reports. They're making it appear that your dad was shot in the crossfire during the raid. But I doubt whether there was really a raid last night."

"Why would you say that—I mean, what's your basis for doubting?"

"You're a grown-up now and I trust that you are fair-minded. I will tell you then that I was supposed to meet with Kumander Diliman, tonight actually, to discuss the exchange of Efren and Edgardo, if Edgardo is still alive. Diliman wanted me to act as intermediary."

"Why did they come down the mountain one day early then?" Antonio reacted outright without pretending he was surprised by the revelation just made.

"That's baffling me too, son. Something's not right in the logical scheme of things."

"Is Diliman among the dead?"

"I've just come from the Municipal Hall to find out. One of the dead resembles Diliman. He must have been shot in the head. Blood is all over his face."

Antonio still keeps in his wallet the 11-year old news clipping from the Bikol News about the raid. He pulled it out that evening at San Mig Garden and showed it to Salvio. Upon reading it, Salvio could not suppress the disgust in his face, and then the carousel in his mind spun again 11 years back. It was Good Friday in Y-riga.

CHAPTER 20

The town was at a standstill. Y-riga, like any town in the country, practically comes to a halt every Good Friday. Government offices, schools, shops, movie houses shut down for the year's holiest day. It is irreligious to giggle, tune in to loud music, sing (except the Pasyon), party or play. So children can't wait for Good Friday to be over. Not Salvio and Minandro. They have always enjoyed the gaudy festivities of the holiday and loved listening to the *Siete Palabras*, the spiritual reflections of eloquent preachers on the Seven Last Words of Christ. Salvio knew them by heart:

1. *Father, forgive them, for they know not what they do*
2. *Truly, I say to you, today you will be with me in paradise*
3. *Woman, behold your son. Son, behold your mother*
4. *My God, My God, why have you forsaken me*
5. *I thirst*

6. *It is finished*

7. *Father, into your hands I commit my spirit.*

The year before, both of them had wept shamelessly during Fr. Barameda's heartrending delivery of *Consummatum Est.*

It is finished is not a plaint of defeat but an avowal of fulfillment of the redemptive mission of Christ, Fr. Barameda orated. It calls attention, he said, to the Lord's temporal physicality on earth and signals His return to Glory. The Lord has fought the good fight, finished the course and kept the faith, the energetic priest concluded his sermon without referencing the Pauline discourse.

The two boys seemed well aware why they couldn't go to poblacion on that Good Friday because of every thing that was going on. So, they asked to be allowed to saunter in kadlagan after lunch.

"Be back before three o'clock and don't use your slingshots today, it's Good Friday," Salvio's mother reminded them. "Otherwise Ma'am Ymelda would be very upset."

"Should we ask ma if it's ok to go?"

"I think she's very sick. I'll tell her when she gets up, Minandro."

"Who'll be with ma?"

"The two maids are here. I called for them to minister to Madi and Rebecca. We'll also leave soon to see Padi at Lourdes."

The two had other plans however—proceed to poblacion as they had always done every year and be entertained by the rites of Black Friday: the parade of motley-colored, artful or otherwise grotesque *carros*, the floats that carry, among others, the statutes of Maria Magdalena, San Pedro, Maria Salome, Veronica, San Juan, the Dolorosa (the image of the unuttered anguish of the Blessed Mother Mary in black veil); the hallowed procession of the *Santo Entierro*; the solemn sounds of drums, trumpets and trombones played by funeral bands, intermittently punctuated by discordant blare of *matrakas*[16] to drive out evil spirits; the scent of candles, flowers and incense; the variant sight of vendors plying their goods (street-cooked native foods, alcoholic beverages, religious trinkets and playthings); the competition of fraternities and sororities in terms of numerical participation and prayerful showmanship; the display (for home towners) of the latest fashion craze by vacationing college students from Manila for the holiday break; and the swarm of the pious and the unpious that descend from the barrios to the poblacion either in a pilgrimage of a sort to imbibe the spirit of the time-honored religious tradition, to be feted or just catch up on what's happening downtown on *Viernes Santo*.

As a younger boy, Salvio had been particularly amused by the float of San Pedro with a live rooster on board even as he wondered whether the Saint likes cockfighting as much as his father; whereas, Minandro always wanted an answer why the

---

[16] *matrakas*: Wooden clapper

ancient crowd who gathered along the road to Calvary had failed to notice the miracle of the Veil of Veronica with the Holy Face imprinted on it.

It was also last year's Good Friday when Salvio made a dare for Minandro to touch the forehead of the Santo Entierro during the procession. Minandro called it. He wiggled his way through a host of devotees packed around the carro and coming close to it, he was taken aback by the sight of the sorrowful face of Jesus lying in repose, still wearing the crown of thorns, eyes half-open. He thought of backing out of Salvio's dare but weighing the consequences of being seen as a wimp, he decided to go for it. He slipped his shivery hand out of the comfort of his trousers' pocket and reached towards Jesus' forehead touching it, but only very momentarily. A man saw what he did and told him to shove off. He quickly disappeared into the crowd of spectators, looking for his friend. Salvio was right there standing by a street-vendor cart all the while watching his buddy's every step. Minandro finally caught Salvio, his eyes telling him, "Done, now your turn."

Salvio bravely obliged and did exactly what Minandro had just done but was able to only hold the hand of the Santo Entierro before being asked to stand back.

Back to each other, there was a distinct paucity of verbal exchange between them. Salvio was first to break the brief silence.

"I had this weird feeling when I touched his hand. I thought I was about to cry although I was really happy. Did you feel the same way?"

Minandro, both hands in clinched fists, clutching his stomach and visibly still quivering, said nothing, but the look in his eyes positively confirmed Salvio's bizarre encounter.

Salvio gently put his arm around his friend and said, "Let's get out here, let's go inside the church and stay there maybe until the procession ends."

"Good."

When the two, on the way to poblacion, came to that part of the highway by the Lourdes hospital, their excitement together vanished. Salvio's mind turned to the lifeless image of Luis in the canal, throat impaled with an arrow. He reckoned it was time to tell Minandro of what actually took place Wednesday night.

Like Salvio, Minandro was haunted by the man whose life was cut short by an arrow drawn from his bow. At the same time he was all too anxious to know the condition of his father in the hospital. Will pa make it? And who will stop Warlito from hurting us, and other people?

They put off their plan without argument and dropped by the hospital. There they found Antonio sleeping on a bench inside the critical ward and Mr. Palma seated beside the bed of Leo, his back towards the door, apparently dozing off too. Minandro without entering the room visually examined the calm face of his father now breathing on his own and thought he looked better than two nights ago. The boys decided not to let their presence known, left the hospital, returned to the highway and then found themselves proceeding towards the poblacion again.

At the canto, Y-rigueños in town for Good Friday were lining up to pick up a copy of Bikol News from the newsstand. The two boys wondered what the fuss was all about and approached the store to investigate.

They saw the headline reading: **Mayor's brother slain in Y-riga raid. Flag flown half mast for town heroes**. What actually astounded Minandro was a blow-up of two pictures on the front page captioned "Weapons used in the raid": a Russian assault rifle and his arrow.

"LB, let's go to the belfry," Salvio told Minandro. "There's something you need to know."

CHAPTER 21

"I just can't believe this is all happening to us. We both took the life of another on the same day and by the same weapon," Minandro whimpered almost inaudibly after Salvio had detailed his account of Wednesday night. He turned away and rested the full weight of his head on his elbows propped against the balustrade of the belfry, both hands clasping his ears, and then fixed a forlorn gaze as far as into the recesses of Sumagang. Salvio watched in disquiet the demeanor of his friend. For the very first time Minandro noticed the teeny-weeny white cloth fluttering on top of iliyan. It would have been a most anticipated moment of triumph for him and Salvio, but it just seemed not kosher at all to bask in it. He was flustered and wanted Salvio to take charge.

"LB, let's go down and make our confession." Indeed, Salvio took command.

Their eyes met. "Okay," said Minandro.

"Wait," Salvio asked his friend to pause in the middle of the stairs as they clambered down from the belfry. "We haven't done any examination of conscience yet."

"Do we have to? We only have to confess one major, major sin."

"You're right. We will tell the venial ones next time, besides the procession will start in about an hour. Alright, you line up for Monsignor. I'll take Fr. Barrameda. Cool?"

"Okay."

"Bless me father, for I have sinned," Salvio began his confession. The church was almost empty of churchgoers who began to get ready for the Black Friday procession. A couple of family devotees were on the last stations of their *via crucis.*

Fr. Barrameda made a sign of the cross to bless the penitent kneeling outside the confession box.

"When was your last confession?"

"Father, my first and last confession was when I was eight years old. I am now ten going eleven, so that was more than two years ago."

"That's all right, son. But have you examined your conscience before coming to this confession?"

"Father, honestly, no, because I had no time. I mean, sorry father, but this is an emergency."

"That's fine, son. I'll help you recall your sins," Fr. Barrameda seemed a bit irritated. He pushed aside the tiny curtain shielding the screen to see the face of the young penitent. "Now, did you quarrel, fight or hit anyone?"

"Yes, father, I hit someone."

"Did you miss mass on Sundays or holy days?"

"Father, wait, let me explain how I hit someone."

"Hmm, yes, go ahead."

"I hit—I shot someone with my bow and arrow."

"Well, well, how, and when, where?" Father Barrameda's voice turned rather stern.

"I shot him in the neck, last Holy Wednesday, at San Joaquin, father."

"What? And what happened to the person you shot."

"He is dead father."

"Really? What made you do it?"

"He was about to bash my teacher with a rock. So, I shot him."

"Oh my God, do you know the person you hurt?"

"Father, he's dead. I know he's dead."

"I said, do you know him?"

"Yes, he's one of the canto boys, one of Warlito's men."

"Did you tell your parents about this?"

"Not yet, father."

"Have you reported to the police?"

"No, father."

"Are your parents in church now?"

"No, father, they don't go to church."

"They don't go to church, ha? Well, this is what I want you to do. Are you joining the procession, are you—? Listen, don't join anymore. I want you to go home right after this confession and tell your parents about the whole story."

"But can I at least watch the procession for a few minutes, just a few minutes?"

"No, I want you to go home right away and do as I tell you. Understand?

"Yes, father."

"Go now."

"Yes, father but what about my penance?"

"Oh—Pray ten Our Father, ten Hail Mary, and ten Glory Be."

"Yes, father. Thank you."

"God, my God, the Father of mercies, through the death and resurrection of his Son has reconciled the world to himself and sent the Holy Spirit among us for the forgiveness of sins; through the ministry of the Church, may God give you pardon and peace, and I absolve you from your sins in the name of the Father, and of the Son, and of the Holy Spirit."

"Amen." Salvio haltingly made the sign of the cross.

"May the Passion of our Lord Jesus Christ, the intercession of the Blessed Virgin Mary and of all the saints heal your sins, so that you may grow in holiness, and be rewarded with eternal life. Peace be with you."

"Amen."

When Salvio came out of the confessional he found Minandro seated on the front pew alone, his nerves ostensibly chafed.

"Are you done too?" Salvio asked as he approached his friend.

"No, I don't trust Monsignor. He might tell. I'll take Fr. Barrameda too."

"Well, go now. No one's in line."

"Wait, I'm still praying my Act of Contrition."

"How many Act of Contrition have you prayed already?"

"Eight, nine maybe."

"That's more than enough, just go inside the stall now. Fr. Barrameda is—cool, somewhat, and will help you through."

While Salvio was somberly doing his penance, Fr. Barrameda bolted out of the confessional box, with both hands covering his mouth to suppress his laughter. Minandro stood up and came out as well, quite perturbed.

CHAPTER 22

Salvio was fondly watching Frankie and the gang engage in banter with the manager of San Mig. He is often amused by the antics of Frankie who resembles his cousin Efren.

"Let's call it a night. I guess my cousin is not coming," Salvio grumbled with a tinge of touchiness. "Well, anyway, it's only one o'clock," he sort of rationalized. "He's probably concerned one of the boys will recognize him."

"Isn't he coming incognito?" Minandro probed his friend.

"I dunno. I, myself, am not sure how Efren looks now. It's been ten, maybe eleven years ago when we last saw him, remember? But, yes, I suppose he should come in disguise. It's certainly not safe for him and perhaps inappropriate for you too."

"Yeah, yeah, I should know. I'm not just used to it yet."

"You know that the Colegio is abuzz with the scuttlebutt that President Marcos plans to suspend the writ of habeas corpus in the coming days and mass arrest of militants will happen."

"There may be a kernel of truth in that rumor. The last phase of our training at the police academy has been dedicated to rigorous drill in riot control. And rookies will be required to complete a six-month stint in the riot squad before being considered for any other detail."

"These aren't good signs at all. Our journal editor, a KMP, has been missing since two days ago."

Antonio was constrained to butt in, "The KMP is only emotionally equipped to launch a revolution. But tactically, it's a pathetic goose egg. Zilch. Nada. They can't win their struggles with ideas alone. Revolution is essentially physical not theories. Armchair warriors are not true revolutionaries."

"In time they will be. Warlito has driven a handful of Y-rigueños to Sumagang. Now Marcos is serving as the New Pilipino Army's biggest recruiter," Salvio came back with a rejoinder.

"But remember that Marcos is not the system in place which is a good deal larger than him. The system is an age-old monster. The president is at a crossroad at this stage and if he is the WW II hero that he claims to be, he must realize, and I hope he will, that the real fight for his country is now. *Ahora.* That fight is all about taking apart the forces that sustain the rotten system. The big step must come from him even if it means defying Uncle Sam and whipping the business class into line as long as he's empowered by the people. Should Marcos choose to be a scoundrel, he will simply be consumed by such a caprice. He is sitting on a volcano. With two thirds of the population going hungry, it could go off to extinction like Sumagang." The youthful university professor was fluid like his father and unwilling to yield his point easily.

"Go off just like that? My sense is that a little uprising here and there could even be stabilizing. Don't you think so? At least it would keep our ruling elites and the *taipans* awake at night, if not spur the meliorists of them into thinking of real change." Salvio was not coy to take the exchange to a higher plane.

"I don't have any quarrel with that proposition, Salvio," Antonio kindly reciprocated. "Indeed, change happens when status quo defenders are pushed into action by the *vox populi*. Even Pilate was prevailed upon by the *shouts* of the multitude, wasn't he?"

"Absolutely, suppress them into silence and God will even give the stone a voice, turning the obeisant, the servile into men." The college student from the Colegio de San Juan, while in assent this time with Antonio's pontification, was bent on not being outdone in pertinent biblical allusions. But at that juncture Minandro inserted his own thoughts into the conversation.

"Unfortunately, as a man of the law now, I'm supposed to defend the scoundrel whenever he's in Manila; it's just how it works, how the system works." Minandro, the Manila policeman, cut in on what's turning into a philosophical colloquy between his brother and his friend, and without actually addressing anyone but the bottle of San Miguel beer he held up before him like a chalice, he returned to Antonio's thesis to take a late gibe at it. "Sumagang, extinct? No, no way. Its glory is in the eyes of its—of its lover. If you love Sumagang, then it is not extinct. If you don't, then it is. Kaput. Dead. It's just how we look at it. It's all in your heart." Then he emptied the bottle.

Antonio slightly knitted his brows, intimating that the romantic spirit of the somewhat inebriated Minandro flew off a bit on a tangent. Salvio saw a sibling brabble coming so he judiciously preempted any controverting repartee from the professor.

"Well, at least we have a choice, or for that matter Marcos has a choice. Cousin Efren didn't have any," said the still sober college boy. "He was fed into the den by a mere twist of fate. He became a rebel essentially by accident or owing to conditions beyond his power—in much the same fashion that Filipinos have been baptized into the catholic faith by default or sans the benefit of any countermanding belief system."

"But I guess you are well aware that many of our countrymen are left without any choices either but to opt out of the arrangement, i.e., try their luck in another clime or, otherwise, turn the country upside down—*make all things new*," Antonio confidently retorted and quoted the Scripture again.

"Well, Prof, given our state of affairs, how can we ever fulfill what's said in the Revelation—well, a renewal *within* the system?" Salvio was apparently all ready to keep the impression he was making even as Minandro, to give the two a freer rein in their argumentation, took the sidelines.

"I'd say plain patriotism," Antonio poised himself to tackle Salvio's last question. "Even agape, instead of the stark pursuit of self-interest; we also live for others as Fr. Barrameda would pound on often in his scathing homilies. By that is meant also Pauline changeover particularly on the part of the economic elites, where personal goals would be in sync with the national objectives, self-identities entwined with the personhood of the state itself. You see, our industrial base will remain weak if the taipans are content with rent-seeking and self-seeking and no amount of political renaissance, if ever that's possible, will alter the equation sans the patriotic idealism of those endowed with economic wherewithal. We demand the most from them for those without simply cannot give what they don't have. This is a sine qua non for take-off. Moreover, the fortunate ones should take to heart the admonition by Jonathan Swift. Whoever could make two ears of corn, where only one grew before, would do greater service to his country than the whole race of politicians combined. Only when these come together will real and decent means of making a living come by for the disillusioned, the desperados, the least of us."

Salvio made a crooked face and then fell into reflection.

"Let me digress a bit, guy Salvio. How did your cousin get hold of you by the way?" Antonio's question was an apparent attempt to change track. "He made the news in Bikol just recently, for looting a police armory, didn't he? And did he mention anything about—?"

The discourse that was becoming quite stimulating was nevertheless cut short when the club manager climbed the elevated platform at the center of the beer garden, waved his hands to signal his audience to quiet down and made an announcement.

"Ladies and gentlemen, San Mig has a surprise number for you from the house. Well, it is actually a special request of his town mates from those two tables down there in the corner."

The Y-rigueños roared. Frankie, giving a thumbs-up, looked jokily at the table where Minandro, Salvio and Antonio were seated as their town mates cheered and clamored: "We want Minandro, we want Minandro!"

Salvio winked at his buddy and shrugged his shoulders, as if saying, you got no choice LB but rise to the occasion.

"Okay but I need a guitar, or at least, a ukulele. Will you ask the manager if he has one at hand, HB?"

Salvio beckoned the manager.

The manager cheerfully approached their table and asked, "Yes sir, how can I be of help?"

"He needs a guitar. Do you have one, please?"

"Sure we have one for our honored guest," replied the manager. He gesticulated to one of the servers whose eye he caught to get a guitar by strumming his belly.

Minandro ascended the stage hesitatingly first which made his brother Antonio fidgety and Salvio thrilled. He was all set to sing his favorite *The Magic Touch* when a group of customers from another table started to howl, indicating that they won't put up with a *guest* performer from the audience. Minandro was oblivious, his inhibitions having been spirited away by the action in his system of at least seven bottles of San Miguel beer. In fact he was ready for the dramatic—to live up to his agnomen as the *Elvis Presley of Y-riga*. He strummed the guitar as hard as he could to open his act. Then pointing his finger he looked straight, with a stern Monteverde look, to the group, and started the *Trouble*:

> *If you're looking for trouble*
> *You came to the right place*
> *If you're looking for trouble*
> *Just look right in my face*
> *I was born standing up*
> *And talking back*
>
> *My daddy was a green-eyed mountain jack*
> *Because I'm evil, my middle name is misery*
> *Well I'm evil, so don't you mess around with me.*

The table of the raucous group was wordless momentarily. Minandro twisted his lips, threw his guitar around his back, gyrated like Elvis and finished his performance as if he was singing only for Salvio in kadlagan.

CHAPTER 23

The police exploits of Minandro have become a good tabloid copy in Manila. He first gained instant celebrity status when he battled singlehandedly two armed bank robbers at downtown *Escolta*, once the 19th century shopping district of Spanish Manila.

Until about the last 40 years, Escolta had been a fashionable section of Binondo, an erstwhile settlement for the diasporic Chinese, the *Sangleys*, who converted to Catholicism during the Spanish colonial period and intermarried with the natives. The community settlement—arguably the oldest Chinatown in the world—that was at one point allowed some form of autonomy by the Spaniards, became the nucleus of commerce of the capital city, bred many of the county's outstanding political figures as well as the economic elites (the taipans, by most accounts), and even begot the first Filipino saint.

Situated by the Pasig River, a strategic waterway at the heart of Manila, Escolta was not spared by the unrivaled power of the USAAF carpet-bombing the capital and the brutal urban warfare in the Battle for Manila during WWII. General Douglas MacArthur's personal quest to *liberate* Manila brought one of the deadliest bloodbaths and devastations in the war, the human toll alone being on a par with the atomic bombing of Hiroshima. From the ruins of the war, Escolta was rebuilt by the Americans as a financial center, the Wall Street of the Philippines, so-called, but because of the near complete destruction of the city, it has never really regained its old Spanish splendor. Binondo, however, survived as Manila's Chinatown.

Minandro was on the phone with Salvio. "It's a doggone shame my Vice Squad partner won't make it on the first day of our Chinatown beat. He has a family medical emergency. Guy, if you want, we can meet at Plaza Santa Cruz in Binondo. From there we can hoof it together to Escolta. Lunch's on me."

Salvio did not hesitate, sensing the sort of worriment in the voice of Minandro that he has become so accustomed to. "I'll see you by noontime, if the traffic permits. I'll be done then with my last finals, hopefully before eleven."

"From *Intramuros*, just take one of those *kalesas* that hang about by the Colegio, but stay away from Jones Bridge to avoid the jam, HB."

144

"Yeah, I guess. And Guy, no fancy Chinese food for me, please. I'm just craving for *mami* and *siopao*."

"Good. See ya."

While waiting for Salvio, Minandro bought a cluster of sampaguita garlands from a street urchin plying her trade about the plaza. The unclean face and tattered dress of the tiny vendor broke his heart. He remembered his little sister Rebecca whom he has not seen in years. Inside Santa Cruz Church a young-looking celebrant was delivering a homily at the daily morning mass in straight American English. This priest must have been from a Jesuit seminary, he thought. He laid the aromal national flowers at the miraculous icon of Our Lady of Perpetual Help and made his usual petitions. Then the rookie detective said so long by gently touching Mother Mary's hand the way, as a little one, he would his mother's to get himself to sleep. His eyes glistened on being reminded by a letter from her mother telling him not to taint the Monteverde name by being a corrupt policeman.

"LB, I think there's a hostage situation in the bank across. I just saw an armed man holding a terrified woman on the 9th floor."

Minandro was trying on a pair of running shoes at one of Escolta's upscale boutiques when he was alerted by Salvio. The commotion was coming from the Philippine Manufacturers' Bank office building across the street.

The plainclothesman on Chinatown duty leaped from where he was seated fitting a shoe and ran towards the street.

His eyes quickly scanned the building, a prototype of postwar American-style high rise.

His nickel-plated .45 caliber pistol drawn, he ordered a passing tour bus to halt just in front of the bank. He climbed to the rooftop of the bus in a flash and hopped to grab the fire escape ladder of the building and swiftly crawled up. He saw a window crack open on the 7th floor, pushed it wider to slip through it and then disappeared into building.

It was vintage Minandro, but Salvio was still stunned by the suddenness of it all. He was guilt-ridden he didn't do enough—in fact he did nothing—to stop his buddy from taking too much chance. But then he could have not dissuaded Minandro from taking on such a singular challenge of his nascent career in the Vice Squad of the Manila Police Department. He's just at it again, Salvio tried to lighten his guilt.

The crowd of kibitzers down the street was growing attracted by two TV vans that came to the scene to cover the action live. After a while, the throng roared when Minandro reappeared behind the glass window of the 19th floor. He was seen fastening one ring of the police handcuff to a metal rail by the window with the robber's hand manacled to the other ring. The second thug with a gun in his hand got out of the same floor and used the fire ladder to scramble to a higher floor. The audience was gasping. Minandro was in close hot pursuit. The TV cameras were rolling bringing live the highly tense situation to the living rooms of Manila. Some onlookers giggled when one camera focused on the shoes of Minandro.

It was a pair of brown loafer and blue athletic shoes. The chuckling stopped when the robber took a shot at his pursuer. Salvio's heart pounded a hundred times faster. The robber fired at the young officer again. Salvio's legs were about to collapse as he imagined LB being stung by a killer queen bee in the neck. But Minandro, predictably unrelenting, returned fire and the man fell to the ground from the 22nd floor like a limp malapaga.

Except for the frantic throbbing of his chest, Salvio was practically immobile during the entire episode. When it was all over, he found himself in grave reflection on the deathly scene in the dark pit of iliyan. At the expense of this poor damned soul, he was hoping, LB should get over it now. At that same moment, Salvio was himself certain he had quite done as well sorting out his own phantom—the ghost from the gutter of San Joaquin.

The following morning, the banner headline of one of Manila's tabloid was brutal: **Rookie Cop Outpaced Robbers with His Hush Puppies and Saucony.**

Minandro had other brushes with tough criminal elements in Manila that made the headlines. There were comic encounters with crackpots too.

One evening, Salvio and Minandro were en route to downtown Manila aboard a taxi. They just came from a party, supposedly a joint college-graduation party for Salvio and Charles Tuason given by Charles' mother. Salvio and Charles had been rivals for the top honors of their business management class at the Colegio de San Juan. Salvio edged out Charles by a few points but both graduated "with highest distinction." Salvio asked Minandro to come with him to the party. Minandro had given assorted excuses not to go, but he ultimately acceded.

The Tuasons trace their ancestry to the settlers of Binondo (Tuason is a concantenation in reverse of Son Tua to Hispanicize it). They live in one of the old Spanish houses in New Manila, once the enclave of Philippines' Old Money and the taipans. Sonya Tuason, Charles' sister, is the same flat-chested Sonya of kadlagan years.

"Glad you made it, Minandro. I'm quite excited to meet you in person. I'm Sonya of the BITRANCO staff house in Y-riga, still remember?"

"I'm happy to meet you too in person. Salvio told me about you and your campus activism."

"Oh, your friend is very sweet. He's been to our house a couple of times already. He gets along well with mom who is also a Bikolana. Know what, I want you to meet someone, please wait a second." Sonya excused herself, and shortly returned to Minandro.

"Minandro, this is Tricia, Tricia Blancaflor, also of the BITRANCO staff house in Y-riga, remember?

"Hi, Tricia."

"Hi—Guy, Elbeeh or Minandro? Umm, please don't be astounded with that, we were also privy to all those shrieks that Salvio heartily filled kadlagan—hahaha. We had even pictures of your tree house."

"Oh yeah?" Minandro, losing his bearing at that juncture, started looking around for Salvio among the crowd in the pool area. But as one of the stars of the party, Salvio had been occupied. So, Tricia babbled nonstop and Minandro had a long night.

"You should have told me that Tricia would be in the party too, HB." Minandro inside the taxi was trying to hide his prickliness but he still came off vexed. "She's very pretty, don't get me wrong, but I'm not really comfortable being with her. I just think her manners are too elitist. We are plebes, *masa*, lest we forget."

Salvio saw his friend's deprecation of themselves as just another display of childish contumacy, but if it was as well meant to define him, he would not hesitate to acquiesce in it. Without forgetting his indigenous beginnings, the *plebeian* appellation in fact came across to him as quite charitable. Besides, he was at that moment too sober and blithesome to be annoyed. He was starry-eyed: She gets lovelier every time I see her. Does she like me? Is Salvio Bartolome good enough for a Sonya Tuason? Education is power, he comforted himself with his father's mantra. And with a diploma from a Dominican private college, inscribed with highest honors, he was also taken up with ponderings about his personal quest—of scaling the next sierra ahead of him, sooner than later.

149

"Believe me LB, I didn't know either," Salvio tried to explain without addressing what to him was Minandro's impertinent aside; he didn't want to ignite a debate. "Apparently, Sonya and Tricia have remained inseparable. That's the plain reason she was in the party without me knowing it. Nothing rocketry at all, LB."

"Sonya is the sister of your classmate, that I know. Are they all cousins?" Minandro was still undeservedly surly.

"Their fathers used to be BITRANCO bosses, that you know. I learned tonight that Sonya and Tricia go to the same school, at La Consolacion College. And as birds of a feather, they stick together. Friends are just like you."

At that point Minandro ordered the taxi driver to pull over. Momentarily Salvio thought that was because of something else until he realized the off-duty policeman had spotted a man exposing himself in front of a ladies' dormitory along the University Belt of Manila. Minandro swiftly alighted from the taxi and pounced on the maniac. The man hurriedly zipped his pants and demanded that he be let go. He claimed he is a police officer patrolling the area and showed his badge. Minandro said policeman or not he is being apprehended for indecent exposure in a public place.

"What indecent exposure," the man complained, "look at me, what am I exposing?" and attempted a sucker punch at Minandro. Minandro saw it coming, ducked and tackled the man. That took away the gleesomeness from the fresh college graduate who came to his buddy's succor by pure impulse and grabbed the man's neck with his forearm. With the man thus hamstrung, Minandro unzipped his pants and pulled his penis out. "This is what you are exposing in public, got it, Mr. Officer?" A photo taken of the exact compromising pose by one lady from the dormitory found its way into the front page of a Manila tabloid the next morning. The banner: **Cop Flasher Caught in the Act; Exhibit 'A' Seized.**

There was one accomplishment which earned Minandro a special presidential award. It happened just before President Marcos placed the Philippines under martial law. In 1972, Minandro, already an old hand of MPD's Anti-Narcotics team, was tasked to apprehend Delfin Ang, a drug lord who was at the helm of a powerful narcotics ring. Ang, a second-generation Chinese born and raised in Binondo, maintained an army of goons that included rogue policemen and military men. His crime syndicate was believed to have virtually more wherewithal than the Philippine Drug Enforcement Agency and had in its payroll influential politicians, trial lawyers, prosecutors and judges. The team raided a drug laboratory run by the syndicate. The operation netted 50 kilograms of heroin and resulted in the apprehension of eight drug traffickers, a chemist and Delfin Ang. The team leader was bribed to overlook the evidence and let go of Ang. Minandro was offered a bribe too in the amount of $50,000.00. He took it and went straight to the prosecutor's office to bring a criminal complaint of corruption of a public officer. The judge who handled the case was also on the take and dismissed the case outright on a supposed technicality. But

Minandro was relentless. A week later, he followed a lead from a mystery informant and discovered a heroin laboratory concealed in one of the Delfin Ang's mansion in a Manila suburb. Minandro and two rookie agents barged into the mansion. When the drug lord attempted to repel his arrest, Minandro gave him no more quarter. He shot him between the eyes.

The Marcos government found out a "Manila Connection" in the trans-Pacific traffic of heroin to the West Coast that was abandoned as a result of the raid breaking up the Manila syndicate. For weeks, the boldness of the manner the raid had been carried out without any warrant sparked controversy in the Manila press over the proper office of the *rule of law*. But, for the most part, Minandro won wide praise.

Salvio, now a junior bank executive, was in the audience as Minandro's special guest at *Malacañang*. The ambiance in the reception hall of the presidential palace was awe-inspiring. Salvio appeared like a doubting Thomas who couldn't believe he was about to be a witness to the honors LB would be receiving from President Ferdinand E. Marcos. But the handsome Philippine strongman, whom theretofore they have seen only seen on television, indeed came out of one of the doors of the Heroes Hall, all smiles, and straightway asked: Where's the crackerjack cop that everyone is talking about? Minandro acknowledged Marcos by smiling back, bowing his head. Salvio was benumbed by the experience. The select audience applauded. As if to suit a manly occasion, Marcos even sounded informal when he delivered his extemporaneous speech. First, he had spent some time bragging about his *heroism* during the war but then humbled himself by comparing his guerilla feats with Minandro's police achievements. In a solemn gesture, the President of the Philippines bestowed on the "brave and honest Manila cop" the presidential medal. Salvio had never been so proud of LB. He was teary-eyed as he joined the warmhearted applause of the well-wishers present during the ceremony. Minandro, looking past and beyond the enigmatic figure in front of him, both reviled and revered by Filipinos, and toward the seal of the Republic hanging on the Palace wall, snapped a firm salute. Salvio came to full attention too and whipped out his own.

CHAPTER 24

The Y-rigueños were not to be outdone. A year following the Malacañang award ceremony, the Y-riga city council passed a unanimous resolution to confer one of the Warlito Magbanua Awards upon Minandro Monteverde during the Silver Anniversary of the City's foundation. Mayor Magbanua covertly lobbied for the resolution as he was angling to ride on the popular esteem of Minandro in his planned electoral bid for the office of the governor. The news spread quickly and Mrs. Monteverde was overwhelmed with congratulatory praises. Rebecca too received cheers from the staff of Lourdes Hospital where she worked now as a nurse. Mrs. Monteverde assumed that Antonio would also be home for the occasion, so she looked forward for a long overdue family reunion. She has not seen her sons since the funeral of Leo who died three years ago and a week after his third book had been published. But Salvio was ill at ease with the news about the award.

From his corner office at the 65th floor of Philman Bank Towers overlooking Laguna de Bay and the skylines of Makati, the bustling modern financial center of the country, Salvio found himself ruminating in front of the tinted glass curtain-wall. The exhilarating panorama freely appreciable from that privileged spot of the soaring concrete tower often bestirs the youthful bank senior VP to savor the treasured iliyan memories of his boyhood. He has gotten used to the ordered chaos of the urban forms, the complex city network and the poetry in the fast lanes, but from time to time he would yearn for the dawdling imageries of the solitary highway, the pristine scenery of the lowlands, and the green plains in the valleys of Sumagang, all affirming the placid air of unsophistication of his hometown. Too often too, the sensation of blissful nostalgia pumps him up and even soothes him whenever faced with difficult corporate issues.

The reverie was interrupted by a sigh. Salvio returned to his desk, jotted down something on a piece of lined yellow paper and then decided to phone Minandro.

"Guy LB, congratulations, yay," Salvio greeted his friend jokingly. "Are you going home for the award?"

"Yes, HB," Minandro, on the other end of the line, replied without any hesitation. "In fact, I had the draft of my acceptance speech done last night. Care to run through it?"

"Hmm—sure. Send it in." Salvio, although a tad surprised, answered. "I'll call you back then as soon as I can—or would you rather join me at The Penthouse tonight?"

"Why not San Mig, for old time's sake."

"Deal. I'll ask Frankie to join us."

The manager recognized Minandro and offered the Executive Room. "My old spot is fine," Minandro declined.

"Excuse me, Captain." Frankie pulled the chair for Minandro.

"Don't do that please, Frankie boy," Minandro chided his town mate for stooping to him.

"Okay, *pare ko.*[17] Sorry."

"How's everything with you, guy Frank?"

"I'm fine, guy Minandro."

"Still working—plying your taxi?"

"Yup."

"Thanks for coming."

"You have the speech, LB?" Salvio asked Minandro right after all three of them had been seated.

"Yeah, here," Minandro handed to Salvio a neatly folded paper he pulled out from his shirt pocket.

Salvio unfolded the paper excitedly. In a few minutes, his face turned serious. He cast his gaze at the electric fan spinning noisily on the ceiling and then nodded slowly but repeatedly as if in agreement.

"Guy, I decided to come and see you because I have also something very important to tell you," Frankie interrupted respectfully.

---

[17] *pare ko:* My friend

"What is it, Frankie boy?" Minandro asked.

"Efren has been sending me feelers that he wants to surrender but only to you, Minandro. The central command has charged him with the mission to beef up their death squad in Manila. More blood will be shed. He said he is tired of it, very tired. He just wants to live a normal life. He is willing to execute a loyalty pledge but no fanfare."

Salvio was beseeching guardedly, and as if initiating those peace moves again during their childish quarrels, he conveyed his plea for long lost cousin Efren—but only in unvoiced silence. He appeared as though he had known beforehand what was to come out from Frankie.

"Alright," Minandro paused, and yielded. "I'll try to talk to Mayor Arsenio and see if he could help get from Marcos a special amnesty for Efren."

Both Salvio and Frankie felt relieved and assured.

"Now, how's the speech, guy HB, good?"

"Perfect, buddy. I thought you would do it but I'm still anxious of the potential consequences. Quite anxious.

CHAPTER 25

"First, I was the informant who tipped off on the drug lord. He had been on our watch for months. He was at the top of our hit list." Efren began his story after all the nostalgic pleasantries.

"How did you survive, why did you not try to escape and what made you become and remain a rebel?" Salvio queried his cousin impatiently.

"They made me a rebel but I chose to remain." Efren heaved his chest. "Let me explain."

"Yes, please, but relax, guy, everything is fine," Minandro tried to becalm Efren.

"There was no raid in Y-riga in 1957. The NPAs were in the poblacion to free Edgardo from his captors. There was no plan to conduct a raid. Snatch Edgardo as effortlessly as possible was the plan. Apparently Warlito and the canto boys got wind of it so the firefight that ensued became inevitable.

The suspicion was that Padre Jacob was the mole because he volunteered to stay in the mountain during the operation. But Kumander Dilim, Rudy and Leila, the leadership of the Sumagang arm of NPA, were killed during the fighting. So Padre Jacob assumed control of the group. He happened to be gay and made me his sex slave for years until one day I slit his throat. The People's Court found my act justified. Then I was made to undergo a painstaking re-education. But in no time, I became a true believer of the movement."

Everything hushed for a while and then Minandro asked: "Are you still a believer?"

"I was. I wouldn't be talking to you now if I still am. The movement however will continue to thrive as long as the vast majority of Filipinos suffer from the injustices of the system and those who have the power to do something about it refuse to understand their plight and pain."

"Guy, injustice is everywhere, as much as justice."

"What is justice to you, guy Minandro, or injustice for that matter?"

"You tell me, guy Efren. Which one are you running from?"

"An eye for an eye is a better individual justice than what Judge Torda dispenses in Y-riga. But when only the privileged few get a free lift and frolic down the slope while the daily grind of the rest is to clamber up every single day as if there is no summit to their tedious and monotonous journey, social justice is compromised."

Both climbers appreciated the analogy but Salvio was quicker on the draw to retort: "Is violence justified to get your own free pass?"

"That's where I began to question the logic of the movement. I suppose the depth of its analysis about the causes of the many ills of our country is foolproof but I'm not sure anymore if the means it employs is the only pathway toward the good society. For example, Minandro, you are also in our hit list. Is that really necessary, or justified?"

"Who killed Captain Jaro, my team leader of the Anti-Narcotics unit?" Minandro followed up without being bothered by the information concerning him just volunteered.

"Our hit squad did."

Minandro squinted and tightened his lips but before he could ask another question Salvio cut in.

"Cousin, do you know whatever happened to Edgardo; he was a KMP trusted by the rebels?" Salvio guardedly inquired. "Nothing was really heard of him after his abduction by Warlito's men. And, what we know is that after the *raid* he was not found either to be in Warlito's quarters at the Cagayunan Bldg."

"Yes I know. We stumbled on his remains in iliyan, in 1960 if I recall correctly. We first thought that the Agtas killed him because there was an arrow in the pit where his corpse was found. But his skull had visible signs of gunshot wounds."

"How sure are you the remains was Edgardo's?" Minandro jumped into it right away.

"Kumander Danny, his classmate at Ibana College, recognized his favorite jacket. Edgardo's student ID was also intact in his wallet."

Minandro and Salvio stared at each other without blinking, or winking.

"Something's not right, cousin? Guy Minandro—? Well, anyway, there's something more you need to know Minandro. Mayor Magbanua had masterminded your father's shooting. His personal bodyguard, Tomas, defected to the NPA three years after the shooting and told us everything. Warlito and his henchmen bungled the execution of the mayor's plan to liquidate Mr. Monteverde. Unfortunately, Tomas was killed last year in one of our encounters with the military in Sumagang."

CHAPTER 26

Minandro prefers to take the nine-hour travel from Manila to Y-riga by BITRANCO bus. He likes the natural wilderness along the roadway which reminds him of kadlagan. But as chief of the Anti-Narcotics Division of MPD, he has more responsibilities now that take up his time. So, for the first time, he took the 45-minute Philippine Airline flight to Naga City, the closest airport to Y-riga.

Within minutes of being airborne he recognized Mt. Isarog and the forest range that connects it to Mt. Sumagang. Iliyan was lost in the green cover by the altitude the airplane gained. That's the dumb explanation for why kadlagan was nowhere to be seen from iliyan. He grinned boyishly. Now, peering down across the landscape with an eye of a soaring eagle gave him an odd sense of conquest over the mystique of Sumagang. There are other ways of reaching the summit, he thought. One could actually come down to the highest peak of the mountain just when as a SWAT officer he had been dropped off by a chopper on one of Manila's tallest structures. The rumination was interrupted. "We will land in fifteen minutes," the pilot announced from the cockpit.

Two military men in full battle gear guarding the tarmac saluted Minandro as he walked toward the terminal. He could only acknowledge the greeting with a nod and smile; a fully packed rucksack was slung on his right shoulder while carrying with the same hand a heavy duffel bag. Inside the bag was his favorite handgun, a gift from Manila Mayor Arsenio. A man offered the service of his mini van as soon as Minandro stepped out of the airport building.

"I can take you to Y-riga, captain," the man was smiling ear to ear.

"Five-hundred is fine with you?"

"More than enough, sir."

"Let's go then."

The driver was visibly excited to have the celebrated policeman on board. As they hit the highway, he was eager to strike a conversation with his passenger who appeared engrossed with something. He gathered his mettle and respectfully said: "Sir, pardon me for being forward but you really looked now a lot more like your father in person than on the newspaper. We, Bikolanos, are really proud of you."

"Thank you." Minandro acknowledged the polite intrusion. "Are you from Naga?" Minandro asked not so much to carry on the conversation as just to return the courtesy.

"No sir, I'm from Bantog but my wife is from Y-riga. She was a student of your father."

"Do you know my father, I mean, personally?" Minandro was lured.

"Yes, sir. I was at the funeral of Mr. Monteverde to pay my respects."

"How well do you know my father?"

"Well, I served as one of the couriers of the Kanlaon unit during the Japanese occupation. He was our role model of a true grit. I guess you got it from your father, sir. He survived all the dangerous missions he had carried out. It's really a shame a genuine hero was felled by bullets not meant for him."

Minandro was muted for a while, and then, his heart throbbing, the confession of Efren rang out in his mind. *Mayor Magbanua masterminded the shooting of your father.*

"Please turn off the air and just roll the windows down. I miss the fresh soothing provincial breeze here," Minandro finally said something.

"Yes, sir." All the windows were rolled down.

"Okay, great." The policeman fidgeted in his seat.

"I'm not sure if Ma'am Monteverde still lives in San Nicolas. Am I taking you somewhere else?"

"We don't own the house anymore." Minandro's focus was diverted. "It was sold after the funeral. Too many memories, my mother said. She's now retired and lives with my sister in San Antonio."

"I see."

164

"What's your name?"

""Fredo, sir."

"Fred, proceed to the New Y-riga Hotel instead, I'm booking there with my friend who is coming from Manila this afternoon, and then take me to the cemetery afterward."

"Will do, Captain Monteverde."

"When you take the turn just before our *old* house, please slow down."

"Yes, sir."

But instead, Minandro asked to stop the vehicle in front of the house, and to linger there for a while. The decorated Manila cop felt a sharp pang of loss. The arching kalachuchis, the giant santol, the hanging orchids, the chicos, the starfruit trees are gone. The boys' room is gone. The Monteverde residence is now a box building serving as a warehouse for Mr. Kiong's flourishing business enterprises. A precious third of Minandro's life-story is now unceremoniously condensed and confined by the four corners of the narra door, the only recognizable relic of his youth that has seemed to remain a priceless gateway to the new structure. For a moment, Minandro wondered whether the door still creaks. His handsome face beamed a simper as the day of the assault of iliyan crossed his mind and then he unleashed again a sigh of wistfulness.

Time to move on.

"Did you say something, sir?"

"Yes, let's move on," Minandro directed the driver.

"Yes, sir."

"What's your name again? Sorry, I didn't catch it earlier."

"Fredo, sir."

"Fredo, you can take your time—I mean, move leisurely from here up to Cagayunan, okay?"

"Sure, sir." He fully understood what his passenger wanted.

"*Mabalos.*[18]"

Minandro had no time to appreciate during his father's funeral the many changes that had taken place in Y-riga after his prolonged absence. But even the measured tour on the highway was still too fleeting to fill in the yearning for the long and rich memories of boyhood in his town.

"Hmm, sir, excuse me sir—do you have a calling card?" Minandro's woolgathering was brusquely interrupted. "If you don't mind, spare me one, a signed one, please. It will come in handy if I get pulled over by the highway patrol."

"No problem. Let me sign this first—here, take one."

"Thank you very much, mabalos, sir." Fredo, the driver, was still sporting a wide smile. "Will you also please sign your autograph on this paper, right below your picture?" He showed to Minandro an old issue of the Bikol News after rummaging through the side pocket of the car. The front page had the picture of President Marcos donning a medal on "the Bikolano police officer." Minandro obliged. The picture

---

[18] *mabalos:* Thank you

of Marcos was crossed out several times, Minandro noted but did not bother to ask why.

"Ma, I'm in town already, but I'm staying in the hotel for security reasons. Three of my men have been here ahead of me. Salvio will be coming tonight." Minandro informed his mother on the hotel phone. "Please say hi to Rebecca for me if she's there. Anyway, I'll see you in an hour to tell you something important about the awards tonight."

"Are you not dropping by the cemetery on the way here?"

"That's where I'm going after I hang up, ma. There's no other time as a matter of fact because I will take the early flight tomorrow to catch a ten o'clock meeting in the morning with Mayor Arsenio."

Mrs. Monteverde realized her son is an important person now. "Don't go anywhere else then. We do have plenty of things to talk about."

"Yes, ma."

"You know that Antonio cannot come. He's defending his doctoral dissertation tomorrow also."

"I know, ma."

Mrs. Monteverde had a lump in her throat. Childhood could be as fleeting as life itself, she reflected. Have we worked hard enough, loved them enough? We raised them as good students, great sons, but heroes? We just tried our best to keep them on their toes, but they make themselves heroes.

"I said the novena for Antonio last night. And of course for you too. How's your Salvio? Well, give my regards to your friend if I don't see him anymore."

"Salvio is doing great, and you will see him tonight."

"Good. Very good. I cooked your favorite *estopado*, by the way."

"Oh yeah? Mabalos, ma. See you later then." Minandro noticed her mother sounding a bit older but still zippy.

"Fredo, wait for me at the lobby." Minandro decided not to rouse his men yet. "I'll take a walk to the church to see our parish priest. I'll be back in a few, then we will go to the cemetery; from there you take me to San Antonio."

"No prob, sir."

CHAPTER 27

The town was in full attendance. It was the first time the Foundation Anniversary of Y-riga, the *Tinagba* Festivals and the Warlito Magbanua Awards Night were to be celebrated on the same occasion. Early in the day the hoi polloi had been treated to an extravaganza of street dancing, military parade, cultural shows and marching band competition to commemorate "the deliverance of the Y-rigueños from the wrath of Sumagang in 1614," when it last erupted. Now, the town's haute monde was all geared up for the evening gala ball that would follow the awards program. The "Sons of Y-riga" to be recognized were Senator Edwin Vinzons and Captain Minandro Monteverde. Senator Vinzons, a former actor and TV host, brought with him a retinue of movie and television personalities as well as media people from Manila to cover the event. The senator was being bruited to vie for the presidency when Marcos would be term-limited. It was this whole shebang that was generating great excitement among the matrons of Y-riga. They couldn't afford to miss the party.

Salvio and Minandro had no time to meet up in the day, so both decided to come early to the Municipal Building to *size up* some things. Minandro's informants got wind of the Mayor beefing up his security for the evening. Minandro on the other hand wanted Salvio's executive input into his plans. All dressed up, Salvio arrived ahead and before going upstairs to wait for Minandro, he gingerly pried into the covered social hall, where the night's affair would take place, located on the street level just beside the building. He was impressed by the entire preparation the town put in. An evening fit for a queen. A welcome streamer for the honorees served to fill out the background of the stage, a beautiful mural of Mt. Sumagang. Then Salvio took one flight up leading to the Main Entrance Hall of the building and surveyed the gallery. He was drawn to the various artifacts hanging around the wall. One particular piece took his attention. He approached it with trepidation. It was an arrow inside a glass frame, the description: "Fatal Weapon Captured in the Raid of '57." It blew him away. Unawares, the reflection of Luis came on the glass alive but skewered by the arrow in the throat. Salvio stood frozen, cold beads of perspiration started to form on his forehead. He thought he had been over it a long time ago. But no, the imagination went awry and the death scene in the gully of San Joaquin came back as clear as yesterday and it so horrified him he didn't even realize Minandro had been there already standing back and watching him. Minandro was himself similarly aghast, if only for the fact that the arrow displayed in the frame was actually his, the weapon which finished off the mean rimoranon that almost killed Salvio.

"It's alright HB. It's gonna be fine after tonight. It's gonna be fine." Minandro put his arm around his buddy.

"You think so, LB?" The dapper bank executive gave his buddy a troubled stare, apparently looking for more honest reassurance.

"Yes."

There was no time to hash out Minandro's daring plan to apprehend and haul up Mayor Magbanua to Manila—dead or alive.

The street vendors had been ready, their stalls and wares in place, before the Panchito Blanca orchestra, the town's best, played its opening repertoire. The handsomely garbed Four Hundred started to trickle in, their status determined for the most part by how late they arrived. The great unwashed of Y-riga took their best spectator spots on the concrete railings enclosing the social hall.

Mrs. Ymelda Monteverde had two "reserved" seats on the front row, one for her and another for a guest of hers. But Mrs. Alvarez took the second seat. "Excuse me, Mrs. Alvarez," Ymelda said, "but this seat belongs to my son's guest. My son is one of the honorees tonight. Don't you see it right there?" Ymelda pointed to the streamer in front of them.

The matron stood up and moved away muttering "well, sorry" without acknowledging Mrs. Monteverde.

Salvio saw what happened and came up to her former teacher smiling. The now sixtyish Mrs. Monteverde looked gorgeous in her *patadyong*.[19]

"Thanks for saving my seat, ma'am," Salvio said extending his arm offering a handshake to Mrs. Monteverde.

Mrs. Monteverde smiled back warmly to Salvio, her eyes beaming as if to tell, Hey, please don't mention it, but aren't you the young man who saved me from great harm years ago? She gladly took Salvio's hand and gripped it as hard as she can. Salvio embraced Mrs. Monteverde in return. It certainly helped to salve his bout with guilt only moments ago.

"Tonight is the culmination of the tenth annual harvest of the seeds of heroism first planted by Warlito Magbanua." Mayor Rufino Magbanua began his commemorative speech.

"The siege of Y-riga actually took place 12 years ago on a Holy Wednesday when Warlito and 13 other Y-rigueños defended our town from the marauders that descended from the mountains. Their martyrdom was the *first harvest*, the Tinagba, if you will, of peace, and spelled the road to perdition of people who might have gotten up from the wrong side of the bed one morning and then turned their frustration against us and our long-held values and beliefs.

---

[19] *patadyong*: A native formal dress

Today, a splinter group of these hooligans still take advantage of the munificence of Sumagang. But they are largely dissipated, they have no place to go and their days are numbered.

"We relive the tradition of supplicating for blessings from the same spirits that guided and protected our ancestors in their struggles against the elements and their enemies. The annual Tinagba ritual of offering and rejoicing symbolizes the reciprocation of every fortune so bequeathed our beloved town."

The TV camera rolled and captured the mayor's gift for soapbox oratory that has earned him three consecutive terms as mayor of Y-riga. Mayor Magbanua was evidently on a campaign mode and set to captivate the townspeople as well as the evening's guests from the capital. The camera spanned and caught the emotions of the crowd and Senator Vinzons waving at them to acknowledge the occasional handclapping. In the front row, Mrs. Ymelda Monteverde and Salvio Bartolome were patiently enduring the fatuity that was transpiring. Father Barrameda, Y-riga's new parish priest, was seated beside Dean Salvador Palma on the same row, both looking expectant of something troubling to take place soon. Minandro's men strategically stationed themselves around the social hall closely monitoring the movements of the Mayor's bodyguards.

Side-glancing at Father Barrameda, Mr. Palma mumbled the exact words Mayor Magbanua had just said in his speech: "We relive the tradition of supplicating for blessings from the same spirits that guided and protected our ancestors." He was audible enough for Mrs. Monteverde and Salvio to give their ears to. "Rufino is not suggesting that Tinagba is somehow also a revival of tribal belief system, or of animism, for that matter, is he?" Mr. Palma was trying harder to entice Father Barameda into a sidebar conversation.

The priest, although not eager, obliged, carefully pacing his words. "Religious beliefs, whether simple or complex are also replete with social elements and actions that often work in a roundabout way." Then the churchman proceeded to up the ante. "You see professor, their primitive rites were meant to excite them and instill collective mental states in the tribes. Our ancestors by obeying their gods allowed them to face the world with a heightened sense of vigor. Our tribal society had then built the capacity to set up itself as both sovereign and divine. Religion as you know is an indispensable force, an essential ingredient, in fact I'd say the *sine qua non,* of society."

Salvio, who theretofore had been straining to multitask between listening to Mayor Rufino Magbanua's speech and thinking through what Minandro might actually carry out, was now all ears to the spinoff dialogue between the parish priest and the college dean. The young banker was stunned by Father Barrameda's somewhat esoteric but frank discourse which he grasped effortlessly. He recalled at that very juncture the simpleminded account of his father, Don Patricio Bartolome, about the religious beliefs of Y-riga's indigenous people, their people, and their worship of Mt.

Sumagang, a narrative that to him is no different from what the Catholic priest had just expounded. Mrs. Monteverde, a little bit hard of hearing, could detect the sound of bickering on the sidelines but, unable to perceive its clarity, dismissed it as the impolite exhibitionism of self-proclaimed savants just like the frequent recondite squabbling between her late husband Leo and Pading Sal of the old.

Mr. Salvador Palma looked smart enough to assure himself as to where Father Barrameda was precisely treading on. But, while still keeping his subdued tone, he sounded losing early in what's turning out to be an intellectual jousting. "You are not being serious father, are you? With due respect, do you realize that your hushed pretenses rang out as plainly maladroit or, otherwise, you are just painfully being heretical, even amateurish like—like booklouse Edgardo, my student of former times, if you remember." Without mincing his words, Mr. Palma thought he could unhorse Father Barrameda by stretching the comparison already made. "Ah, that poor kid Edgardo, may he rest in peace, but as cerebral as he was, so was he just as ludicrous in persuading me once that our national flag and god could be somehow exchangeable."

"Yes, I remember Edgardo. He also visited my confessional not to tell his sins but to posit and test such a proposition. A very promising young man, nonetheless." The priest calmly parried the counterstroke being launched by the professor. "Now let me put it this way, professor. And please let's be civil and listen to the speaker on the platform after this." Father Barrameda, stern and firm, stepped up to a higher plane. "Look, our ancestors ascribed divine attributes to Mt. Sumagang not so much because of its enduring physical magnificence as by what it symbolized to them that distinguished their tribe from those tribes that worshiped Mt. Isarog or Mt. Mayon, for instance. It was, to them, therefore a representation *both* of their *god* and their tribal *society*. Absent the identifying festivities and rites, occurring at more or less regular interludes and affirming the *sentiments of the collectivity*, the esse, the very being of the tribe, was liable to disintegrate."

"Wow, I'm just befuddled now. Don't you think it should be me, whom everyone calls the 'commie' professor, who should be burbling all these things, these unorthodoxies?" Then, Mr. Palma, turned pharisaic on the sly. "Anyway, father, if we follow your thesis, how do we distinguish at this point Good Friday from Tinagba?"

Father Barrameda purposely allowed the professor's question to linger. Meanwhile, more buoyant and confident on the stage and visibly inspired, Mayor Magbanua rambled on. "On this singular occasion, we commemorate the heroism of the 14 Martyrs of Y-riga by conferring the Warlito Magbanua Award upon other well-deserving Y-rigueños who have become role models of valor or exemplars of exceptional achievements. It is the highest award this town bestows upon its sons and daughters who have acted beyond the call of duty or attained excellence by sheer mastery of adversities." The Y-rigueños gave an extended applause to their impassioned mayor.

Remaining poised and unaffected, Father Barrameda likewise picked up from the mayor's lines just dispensed and serenely slipped through the pharisaical entrapment calculated by Mr. Palma. "Look, are these in their spirit, are these real sentiments?" the priest demanded, waving his right hand confidently in an open palm gesture as he would do it from the pulpit. "Do you see all these activities that we are witnessing as a remaking of those ancient sentiments?" After pausing momentarily, Father Barrameda pressed on to challenge further the professor, this time drawing parallels from the Scriptures. "Do you consider these as *festivals celebrated at their proper time with a sacred assembly* or, even more so, as *the substance of things hoped for?*" The professor's head began to twirl but the clergyman was not finished. "The question, I suppose, that is more apropos is: Can you tell the difference, at least at this point, between the celebration of Tinagba and the commemoration of the so-called martyrs of Y-riga in terms, for example, of their purpose and the outcomes they are designed to produce?"

Mr. Palma realized he might have bitten off more than he could chew and judiciously decided to return his attention to the performance on the stage.

After the long-winded speech of Mayor Rufino Magbanua, the Master of Ceremonies lost no time calling the participants of the *Rigodon de Honor* to come forward and make their dance formation. The choreography was put together by the famous Manila dancing queen Betty Camposano, a native Y-rigueño. Forty pairs pre-selected by Y-riga's Blue Ribbon Committee had rehearsed arduously for their number. But the committee was compelled to make adjustment because of the untimely illness of Mrs. Magbanua, and three pairs from Senator Vinzons' entourage, all movie celebrities, wanted to dance the rigodon.

The mayor who was flanked between Senator Vinzons and Minandro on the stage stood up from his seat and called his guests of honor, "Gentlemen, shall we dance the rigodon? Senator, Captain Monteverde, do you know the steps?"

"Certainly, Mrs. Vinzons and I danced the rigodon at the Malacañang Palace a couple of nights ago."

"And you Captain?"

"Minandro was somewhat caught by surprise but assured the mayor, "Nothing to it, mayor. I'm a natural dancer—I guess I am; besides rigodon routines are simple marching steps, I'll be able to follow." Minandro completed his response wryly and without looking at Mayor Magbanua. His eyes were in fact anxiously roving around looking for Rebecca from the audience.

The mayor took it as a fleck of unease on the part of Minandro and, in a flippant gesture to relieve the distinguished officer of it, politely spoke, "Mrs. Magbanua is indisposed tonight so I'll find myself a partner from the crowd."

Don't patronize me, Rufino Magbanua. I know what wickedness you are capable of, wise guy! Minandro tried to feel the handgun strapped to his leg and then foxily strain his sight to check on the assigned spots of his men.

Rigodon is a stately court dance believed to be of French origin that was fashionable in Europe in the 18th century. An adulterated version of the dance might have been given currency during the late Spanish era by Filipino aristocrats returning from European exile. It is supposed to be performed to lively orchestra music at state functions by important government officials and members of high society dressed in pomp native formal attire. The pageantry has come to be popularized even among ordinary folks but the dance has retained its name as Rigodon de Honor.

The emcee held off summoning the dance participants by name while Mayor Magbanua strolled around the dance floor obviously looking for a partner. Mrs. Alvarez leered at him but the mayor walked past the matron. He stopped in front of Ymelda, bowed and extended his right arm to her. As Minandro was coming down the platform, he saw Rebecca nodding from another row, apparently nudging her mother as if saying, Ma, isn't this what you have always fancied doing? Ymelda stood up gracefully without seizing the mayor's hand but accepting the polite solicitation. Minandro was relieved that he would have his own dance partner out of dear sister Rebecca, so he rushed toward her, but Mrs. Alvarez cut in and clutched his elbow securely. Minandro was nonplussed while Mayor Magbanua, grinning and marveling at the odd couple, indicated he was quite pleased that his guest of honor, the debonair officer, also found a well-primed partner.

The dance troupe was ready, thought the Master of Ceremonies who promptly proceeded to announce the participants. "Ladies and gentlemen, first, the *cabeceras* of the Rigodon de Honor: Mayor Magbanua and his partner, Mrs. Ymelda Monteverde, the honorable Senator and Mrs. Edwin Vinzons, Captain Minandro Alvarez, oh, excuse me, please, Captain Minandro Monteverde and Mrs. Marie Alvarez—"

Salvio was impishly all smiles as he watched his guy Minandro marched to the center of the ballroom with the heavily made-up Mrs. Alvarez proudly gliding by his side, the scent of her timeworn perfume bringing forth some boyhood memory that has gotten to the well-groomed officer. Rebecca came forward to fill the empty seat vacated by her mother and, snickering, twinned with Salvio in his playful mischief.

To the animated rigodon music of the Panchito Blanca orchestra, the dancers paraded and marched, swayed and sashayed, curtsied and flirted, nothing really graceful, nothing intricate, as the town folks surveyed from the concrete railings the who's who of Y-riga, the ladies in pricey gaudy *ternos* or patadyong and the men in their fine formal dress, the barong Tagalog.

"The public may dance," the emcee announced after the rigodon. The orchestra played the English Waltz, or *sinangkaka*, as the masses call it. Eager pairs trooped to the center of the ballroom to join the participants of the rigodon who had not enough of it and chose to go on dancing. Mrs. Monteverde did not wait to be escorted back by Mayor Magbanua to her seat. Rebecca stood up and kissed her mom. "You're so beautiful, ma," Rebecca lovingly complimented her mother. She waved at Salvio and nicely bade him adieu. "See you guys later."

"Where are you going now," Ymelda asked Rebecca as if her daughter was still an impetuous fourteen years old.

"Not with my boyfriend, mother dearest, I don't have one. With the nurses, of course, ma!"

Mrs. Marie Alvarez was smiling winsomely at Salvio while the sinangkaka was being played with gusto by the orchestra, but he was snappier this time to avoid the invitation. Ignored, her facial expression changed, telling her age. She hoisted herself, walked up to the dance floor and began to waltz with no one.

Thankfully back to the stage, Minandro watched the whole show unfold on the ballroom floor. He saw his mother and best friend looking intently at him. Rebecca was nowhere to be seen again.

The audience cheered when Minandro, as the next speaker, was called. He rose to his feet in his white service uniform and matching white Pershing cap, the presidential medal displayed around his neck. The first to accept the award, he was all set to spiel.

"I wish to acknowledge the presence of my mother, Mrs. Ymelda Monteverde, a retired public school principal, and my dear friend Mr. Salvio Bartolome, a native of this town and now a Manila banker. I know my beautiful sister Rebecca is here in the audience. She just prefers not to take the limelight. Hi, sister, wherever you are.

"My mother said I was a late-bloomer in that I had not uttered my very first word until I was three years old. That's why guy Salvio has nicknamed me, LB, meaning late-bloomer. I guess it's been a long journey for me because tonight I have more than a mouthful to say.

"Mr. Bartolome and I grew up in this town together. We were drawn to the heights of the mountains because of our love of it. We know that reaching the peak is not always easy. It demands physical strength, certain experience and planning, sometimes luck, but, foremost of all, perseverance. There are no shortcuts. You rob yourself of the precious moments at the top when you accept the challenge, yet take the easy path. If you summit the hard way, you can gaze proudly across the landscape below with the eye of a victor. I suppose this is true to us as individuals and as a town.

"Fellow Y-rigueños and friends of Y-yiga, let me tell you outright that I cannot accept, yes, I cannot accept, this award—because I still have one great adversity to master, if I may borrow from the wisdom of the honorable mayor. You know, it's alright to go slow to avoid the dark pits and treacherous obstacles. You just have to be ready for these dangers and the surprises along the way. But don't stop. Keep pushing.

"And tonight, I will try to retrace the difficult journey by telling you at the outset that the Warlito Magbanua Award is an aberration, to say the least, maybe like many other things we believe or are made to believe in this town.

"Let me say this, and I'm summarizing the late Leo Monteverde here. The things that we believe, or are made to believe in this town, are not entirely imposed upon us from the outside for the simple reason that even Y-riga cannot exist except through our own individual permission, and therefore these forces can only penetrate us and govern us if we allow them. Accordingly, if we do, and these powers are supposedly part of our collective being, they could energize and inspirit us beyond our individual capabilities. But, what happens when the community fails—and we are left again to our own forces? Back to our individual planes, it is imperative to find other pathways to attain new heights, rise above ourselves, reclaim our power to create our new selfhood, as we remake, rebuild our town."

The insights from Minandro's father that were abstracted by the proud son proved compelling to Salvio and directly seeped into him. They were not in the speech he had gone over, he was sure. The invigorated speaker, he thought, was also making references to him, a full-blooded agta, now an important corporate man, but whose tribe in Mt. Sumagang is under threat of being rendered extinct. *Can I carry the burden?* The idea distressed him. And then the image of youthful Minandro, wearing his gritty Monteverde look, crossed his mind. He saw his determined guy LB, the hotshot of kadlagan, his battered slingshot—not a burnished medal—dangling around his neck, standing in sharp salute to a fluttering torn piece of blanket, the flag they toiled to erect on the peak of iliyan.

The TV camera was perfectly angled on the dashing speaker. Y-riga listened in awe and admiration. Mrs. Monteverde imagined the handsome and eloquent officer on the platform as the three-year old Minandro, tubby, chinky and aphonic, transfigure into a full-grown Leo Monteverde.

Mayor Magbanua, his lips tightening, his mind racing, began to fret. The mayor's bodyguards noticed the labored comportment of their boss. Minandro's own security were watching them watching him.

Father Barrameda, distinctly recalling the brief morning encounter with his visitor in the parish office, was mindful of every word spoken by Minandro, yet quite assured and unquestioning. He shut his eyes in prayerful patter and blessed his flock. May the Spirit of the Lord dwell in us.

Captain Minandro Monteverde took a long pause in his speech. He connected. His audience hushed. Turning even more solemn, he affirmed his oath before his town mates—

I am a police officer, a soldier of the law. I must serve honestly and faithfully and if need be lay down my life as others have done before me rather than swerve from the path of duty. It is my duty to obey the law.

Minandro's face shone and his service uniform brightened up. Salvio witnessed it.

Minandro went on to tell his story, their story, as the camera closed in on him, then on the lovely mural of Sumagang. Salvio was calm and content as his guy LB gazed not skyward but far across and beyond the town's social hall.

EPILOGUE

The 10-year old tradition of conferring the **Warlito Magbanua Awards** was immediately undone by the unanimous vote of the city council of Y-riga.

President Marcos declared martial law in the Philippines in 1972 with the tacit blessings of the United States. He assumed dictatorial powers, incarcerated many of his political opponents and ruled the country with an iron fist for another 14 years. The dictatorship failed to quash the armed rebel movement. It was however a peaceful *people power* revolt that ousted Marcos in 1986.

Mayor Magbanua, a Marcos loyalist, suffered from a fatal cardiac attack on learning that Marcos had been ousted from power by the people's uprising and the Marcos family sent into ignoble exile.

The **New Pilipino Army** thumped its relevance by despising the successful popular revolt and refusing to be a part of it.

Salvio Bartolome reached the peak of his banking career early, at age 35, when he was named the president of the Philippine Manufacturers' Bank (Philman Bank). Unbeknownst to almost anyone, he is the first IP (indigenous people) to hold such a position in a major Philippine bank. All of his siblings became successful professionals in their own right. He married Manila socialite Sonya Tuason with whom he has worked closely on various missions for the underprivileged, the IPs in particular.

Don Patricio Bartolome, at the earnest plea of Salvio, bequeathed all of his Sumagang property to the town of Y-riga to serve as a perpetual reservation site for the IPs of Mt. Sumagang. All of the Bartolome children gladly approved of the bequest. Don Patricio died a happy man.

Efren was granted amnesty by President Cory Aquino who succeeded Marcos. He now works for his cousin Salvio as Chief Security Officer of Philman Bank.

Frankie is blissfully married to his town mate, Letty, the San Mig Garden dancer. Together, they operate a fleet of taxis in Manila.

Rebecca migrated to Mountain View, California where she works as an ER nurse. She married a Norwegian engineer. They have a beautiful daughter whose name is Lea—Lea Monteverde Christensen.

Mrs. Monteverde moved with Rebecca to the U.S. after donating the iliyan property to the Agta settlement of San Nicolas. She is Lea's dear nana and home teacher.

Antonio obtained his Ph.D. summa cum laude at Santo Domingo University. He is completing his second book about *patriotic capitalism* for developing countries.

Mr. Palma ran for vice mayor of Y-riga and lost by a slim margin.

Ibana College created a professorial chair in honor of Leo Monteverde.

BITRANCO was taken over by creditors in 1973.

Mt. Sumagang, according to a study in 2001 by the Philippine Institute of Volcanology and Seismology, is still an active volcano contrary to popular belief. But if ever it would unleash its power again, Y-rigueños will be forewarned, the study concluded.

Minandro Monteverde was in the midst of building a solid case of frustrated murder against Mayor Magbanua when the mayor succumbed to heart attack. After 25 years of service, he retired from the police force. Minandro successfully raised his own family. He still serves as official adviser to the Mayor of Manila on the City's intractable drug problems. He finds meaning in life devoting time doing what he loves doing: writing songs and using the art form to assert a purpose. To him, song is also *power*. He has so far declined urgings from town mates, HB among them, that he run for an elective public office.

*　*　*

You are not cut out for just mountain-gazing from the belfry, Salvio once provoked his friend.

I'm also LB, not for nothing, he shot back.

And HB saw the soul of a true grit in his guy's eyes.

www.ingramcontent.com/pod-product-compliance
Lightning Source LLC
Chambersburg PA
CBHW071203260626
47162CB00003B/1154